Obscurus, 1939
Stuart Drake

All rights reserved copyright2024 Obscurus 1939 Paper Street Books This and all other works under Stuart Bray books are the sole property of the author. This book, short Stuart Bray short stories, or merchandise under Paper Street Books/Extreme F'N horror are not to be replicated, and or copied in any fashion without consent from the author. All characters in this book are purely fictional and are in no way meant to resemble any actual person, Living or dead. All views and opinions expressed by these fictional characters are in no way the actual views or opinions of the author. All images here are property of the owner, and or public domain. For more information about copyright law please visit www.unitedstatescopyrightlaws.gov

Edited and formatted by Jason Nickey (Author of Static, Reckless Abandon, and They come from within)

Self-published under Paper Street Books Inc.

This book is dedicated to my two sons, Mason, and Wade. May you both live the happiest, longest of lives. I love you both more than anything in the world.

"The mining industry might make wealth and power for a few men and women, but the many would always be smashed and battered beneath its giant threads."
-Katherine Susannah Prichard

Contents

Prologue		1
1.	This Empty House	9
2.	Lessons learned In The Cold (Quincy Shoultz)	19
3.	A Shoultz Family Curse (Beatrice Shoultz)	33
4.	The Value Of Copper (Edward Copper)	45
5.	All The Time In The World (Dean and Jeffery)	55
6.	Without Labor, Nothing Prospers (Harold Brey)	65
7.	Such A Quiet Place To Sleep (Miss Nimms)	77
8.	A Light In The Darkness (Henry Shoultz)	87

9.	Necessary Cruelty (Mr. Sinclair)	101
10.	The Silo (Alan Shoultz)	111
11.	I'll Never Forget The Winter Of 1939 (Quincy Shoultz)	127
About the Author		133

Prologue

Quincy fell from the rusty ladder as it shook loose from the cave wall. The fall towards the bottom felt like an eternity; an eternity of fear, and so many mistakes that could have been avoided if only he had stopped to think. The breath knocked from his lungs as his upper-back hit the bottom first. There was nothing there to soften the blow, besides a few patches of dead grass that had not seen sunlight in ages.

From the angle that young Quincy Shoultz found himself, the small beam of light coming through the truss opening looked miles away. His father had always told him and his kid brother, Henry, that the mines were no place for boys his age. Quincy knew this to be true, but like always, putting his own spin on the advice given to him. These mines are not meant for anyone, no matter their age. Instead of spending time on his back, reflecting about the could haves, Quincy needed to find a way out of this cold, blackened hell.

"Quincy, Are you alright?"

Quincy sat up, rubbing the sore spot on his back. Before he could respond to his younger brother up above, a small gust of wind threw coal fines directly into his face.

The sound of Quincy's distress caused Henry to become more frightened than he already was. He stuck his head deeper into the darkness, hoping to catch a glimpse of his older, wiser sibling.

"Henry! I must find my way out of here. You run on up to the front entrance of the mine. Call my name as loud as you can."

Quincy waited, knowing well that it would take a moment for his brother's young mind to process his request. He squinted towards the ceiling, rubbing his eyes, using his equally filthy shirt sleeve. Henry's head had disappeared from the small opening, meaning that he must have begun making his way down towards the mine's entrance. He pulled himself up using an old mining cart that he had luckily missed during his unexpectedly quick trip towards the ground.

Quincy's father had condemned this mine years ago, too many accidents, too many deaths. The new mine was found about five or six miles east of town. Falling down the shaft of the new mine would mean a quick and speedy rescue by one of his father's employees, but that certainly would not be the case in this situation.

"Quincy?" a small voice called out from up ahead. Quincy felt a wave of relief unlike any he had ever felt in his life.

"Henry!" Quincy shouted at the top of his lungs, taking in another mouth-full of black dust. He coughed, leaning over the mining cart in front of him, fighting for even the tiniest amount of clean air.

"Quincy!" Henry shouted again, this time sounding slightly closer than before.

He was not coming into the mine, was he? He was told to stand at the entrance, not to wander irresponsibly inside. Irresponsible, that was exactly what Quincy had been when he decided to climb down that old ladder, when he decided to enter the mine his mother and father had warned him about. And worst of all, dragging Henry into his irresponsible, world eating, black hole of teenage rebellion.

"Henry! Stay where you are! Do not come inside!" Quincy cleared his throat, spitting out what looked like black slugs straight from one of those scary books he had been reading before bed.

"Quincy? It is getting darker and darker. I'm scared I want to go home!" Henry cried out, the darkness wrapping its cold fingers around his body, pulling him in further.

"I said stay where you are! Stop trying to find me. Let me find you. Keep shouting my name!" Quincy jogged towards the spot he had last heard his younger brother, kicking piles of broken pickaxes, ironically bumping into bumper posts, feeling his way along the cold rock walls. "Henry! Henry! Call out my name!"

Little did Quincy Shoultz know, he had heard his younger brother's voice for the very last time. Henry had fallen into a sinkhole, the same sinkhole that had taken the lives of three others before Henry's. By the time Quincy had found the mine's entrance, Henry had been gone for over an hour.

"He got lost in the mine. Henry got lost in the mine while we were playing!" Quincy cried out to his mother as he rushed into their home, his face and clothes blackened, his throat raw from running.

In the days following, Henry's tiny body was recovered from the depths of the sinkhole in the mine. He had fallen over forty feet before hitting the rocks at the bottom. The town doctor said it was an instant death, and that Henry felt no pain during his last few moments alive.

Quincy was never comforted by the doctor's reassurance. He only imagined the fear that his younger brother must have experienced during that fall to the bottom.

Had Henry reached out for him? Had he cried out for his big brother to save him? Even after an entire year had passed, the questions never stopped, neither did the agonizing pain that went with them.

The atmosphere at the funeral was like a dark rain cloud had squeezed itself through the front door, then sat comfortably in the empty seat to Quincy's right. His mother and father both kept straight faces, strongly advising their only surviving son follow suit. It was not from a lack of empathy or caring, it was to show everyone in town that attended that evening that their family couldn't be broken, no matter how significant the loss.

Mrs. Shoultz dabbed under her eyes with a salmon pink handkerchief, while Mr. Shoultz sat as straight as a long piece of freshly cut pine. Those in attendance were mostly shopkeepers and employees from the mine. They had come to pay their respects, but also to see if Mr. Shoultz had broken. The room filled quickly, not a whisper amongst the crowd as they all took their seats, letting the service begin.

Quincy kept his head bowed for most of the service, even after the prayers had ended. The daughter of the hardware store owner noticed this, and wondered if it was guilt that kept the remaining son's head bowed, his eyes pointed towards the tips of his shiny black dress shoes. The shop keeper's daughter would wonder but would never know the truth as to why young Quincy Shoultz kept his head bowed.

"Raise your head. People will think you are weak. We cannot afford to look weak right now. Mourn in the privacy of our warm home when we get there, but not here, not now." Mr. Shoultz placed his hand firmly on the back of Quincy's neck, pulling his head up so that his was forced to look straight ahead.

"I can't look at him, father. I can't remember him like this!" Quincy protested, pulling away from his father's firm grasp. Mr. Shoultz looked embarrassingly around the room, eyes darting away from him, the townspeople pretending not to have seen. "When we arrive home, the two of us are going to have a very long talk about how we are to behave in public."

Quincy knew he would receive a firm lashing later. One that would make sitting on his bottom comfortably a tedious task to say the least. The physical pain would never outweigh the pain he felt in his heart, staring up at the little blonde boy in the expensive casket; the boy he felt responsible for putting there.

"Can I go down to the creek with you? Please, Quincy!" Henry's voice played in Quincy's head like he was sitting just inches from him, still alive, still wanting to run around and play.

"We'll go later. Leave me alone for a minute, will you?" Quincy felt a deep pit of sadness, hearing his *own* voice as well. *Why hadn't I just played with him? Why hadn't I spent more time teaching him all the things I had learned before he was ever born?*

Death had always been served with a side of regret. Young Quincy Shoultz was now learning just that.

Chapter 1
This Empty House

November 1939
Obscurus, Pennsylvania

It was the winter of 1932 in Obscurus, Pennsylvania. Quincy Shoultz stared from the family room window of the giant house his father had built. Quincy never liked the old Silo that sat out beyond the holler. It wasn't that he was afraid of the old town legends he had been hearing his entire life, or the fact that when the moon hit the top of the silo just right, it looked like a giant man standing alone, just waiting to turn and catch whoever was staring in his direction. It was that Quincy had never been *that far* past the holler. Not a single time in his short fifteen years of life. In fact, there were many things young Quincy had not done yet. Living on the outskirts of a town populated with merely twelve hundred people, you were not born with expectations of greatness. Most of the long-time residents of Obscurus had been residents since before the great depression, a depression that left the town crippled, never able to fully recover.

"Some folks take a bit longer to get over loss as great as that. First, the big cities must pull themselves back together, then we will follow," the Shoultz matriarch would add, shaking her head as she rocked back and forth in her chair, sewing a green and red scarf for the youngest of her two children. She never looked up, never missed a single stitch, never once had to start over.

"We are lucky that your father was not affected the same way all those other men were. Your father is a smart man, and he knew there would always be money in the mines. A few men had to be let go, sure. But your daddy has kept a great portion of this town alive, and we should thank him everyday for all the sacrifices he has made for our family."

The Shoultz name was to coal, as Folgers was to coffee. There was not a man, woman, or child in a one-hundred-mile radius that had not at least heard the name in passing, nor were there many who had not been in some way affected by the business decisions made by Alan Shoultz and the army of 'yes men' at his disposal.

"What is over those hills, mother? Is it a farm?" Young Quincy pressed his finger on the cold window facing the snow-covered hills. Beatrice Shoultz stopped knitting, just long enough to look out the window and see the old silo in the distance.

"That is the old farm where your father grew up with his own parents. We bought that land and built our own home on it before you were born. Why do you ask? You have never asked about the farm *before.*"

Quincy turned his head back towards the window, seeing the silo in a different light than he had just a few moments ago. Beatrice shrugged her shoulders before smiling in her eldest's sons' direction, admiring his dirty-blonde hair in the winter light.

"Mother, I'm hungry!" the youngest of the Shoultz children whined, dropping the little wooden train toy that only held his interest for a short while.

"Henry, I told you five-minutes ago that dinner would be ready shortly. You cannot expect Miss. Nimms to rush just because your tummy rumbles."

Miss. Nimms was the housekeeper; she had been even before Henry was born. The Shoultz family had seen their fair share of maids over the years, all of them leaving without notice once they came to the realization that the lady of the house could be a tad much at times.

"Did you even wash these linens? I want them cleaned right, not washed off in the creek!" Mrs. Shoultz would shout, slamming her fists against the wall in anger. Miss Nimms, on the other hand, had learned to block out the sudden outbursts directed at her. She learned early on in life that it paid to just nod and smile, even when an angry, rich white woman was screaming just inches from her face.

"It's always a negro woman. Why on earth do you suppose that is?" Beatrice Shoultz would ask her husband, shaking her head while she watched every new housekeeper scrub the bathroom tile. Alan Shoultz would shake his head and grunt, flipping through the stack of papers atop his home office desk. "Is it something to do with biology? Is it the only work they can find?"

Beatrice would pester her husband until he finally gave her the attention she craved. "It is a financial matter, dear. White housekeepers are notorious during the interview process, always asking for more money than the employer is willing to pay." Mr. Shoultz would clear his throat, then start scribbling away on accident reports handed to him by the supervisors.

"Such a shame." Beatrice would add candidly, pressing down on her dress, trying to get rid of the smallest wrinkle.

The dinner trays covered the overly large red oak table in the dining room. "Yall dig in.," Miss. Nimms would say excitedly, rubbing her hands on the front of her apron.

Beatrice was annoyed by Miss. Simms country twang. Rolling her eyes, hoping her husband at the opposite end of the table would notice. "That will be all." Beatrice waved her hand, dismissing Miss. Nimms back to the kitchen.

"The library in town is closing after the fire last month. They say they haven't the money to pay for the damages." Mr. Shoultz announced as he flipped through the newspaper. Quincy and Henry sat across from one another, making silly faces, trying to get the other to laugh.

"The city doesn't have the money to fix it. It is a public library, it should be a public matter," Mrs. Shoultz added, hoping her husband would engage with her, even for a moment.

Alan Shoultz cleared his throat, flipping to the next page without responding. Quincy was old enough now to notice social cues that he did not quite understand just a few years ago. He had never seen his parents as the quintessential, taking your children on vacation to the beach type, but it was not particularly bad. A small part of him had always known, like he had been born with the knowledge already wired in his brain.

Henry suddenly burst with laughter, putting his hands to his mouth to hold it back.

"That is enough! We do not play at the table!" Mrs. Shoultz snapped, slapping her hand down next to her plate. Henry continued to laugh, doing his best to stop. "Miss. Nimms, come in here please!" Beatrice grabbed the little silver bell she always kept at her side, ringing it to the point that Mr. Shoultz cleared his throat loudly, standing up from the table, and leaving the room.

Miss. Nimms entered through the swinging door. She scurried to Mrs. Shoultz's side, her eyes darting around the room like it was on fire. "Yes madam? Is there a problem with the food?"

Beatrice rolled her eyes, annoyed having to explain the situation. "Yes, please take Henry to wash up, then put him in bed. He will not be having desert tonight."

Hearing the news, Henry began to cry, kicking his feet wildly under the dining room table.

"Yes madam, will do. Come on, now. Let us get you upstairs." Miss. Nimms lifted Henry from his chair. He kicked and screamed even harder, slapping at Miss. Nimms as she exited the room with him tucked tightly under her right arm.

"The headaches you children can cause. It's a wonder I can even think straight in this house."

Quincy lowered his head, feeling terrible about getting his younger brother in trouble. No matter which of the two brothers caused the commotion, no matter which of the two got in trouble, they were *both* scolded by Beatrice.

"I think I have lost the will to even finish this meal. I think I will retire to the bedroom for the rest of the evening. Quincy, you finish your dinner, then head up to bed as well." Beatrice stood up from the table, brushing out the wrinkles in her dress.

Quincy pushed the green beans and mashed potatoes around on his plate for a few moments, the dining room now completely silent, only the sound of silverware scraping the glass plate.

What was missing in this house? Quincy wondered, looking around the giant dinning room, staring up at the rows of China cabinets and the expensive paintings his father imported from Russia. How could a place so big and beautiful feel so lifeless? so empty?

On Quincy's way up the huge winding staircase, through the upstairs main hall, he passed by his mother's bedroom, the door cracked open just slightly. Beatrice sat on the chair in front of her vanity, pulling the pins from her hair, letting it fall to her shoulders.

Miss. Shoultz held her beauty above all else, she had done so her entire life. "How did you grow old so fast?"

she asked herself, placing a hand on her cheek. Quincy kept walking, passing by his father's office on the way to his bedroom. Mr. Shoultz stood in front of a small bar he kept in the far corner of his grand office, pouring a glass of scotch from a crystal bottle. Alan Shoultz was a stern looking man, a full head of black hair, a face like someone sucking on a piece of sour candy.

"Goodnight father." Quincy whispered, just low enough to not be heard.

Inside his bedroom, Henry was already tucked into bed. He stared up at the ceiling, just waiting for his older brother.

"Quincy!" Henry called out with a huge smile.

"Why are you so excited to see me? We were just eating dinner together only fifteen-minutes-ago." Henry expression nonetheless stayed the same.

"I don't know. I'm just really excited to talk about school tomorrow. Aren't you excited?" Henry asked, sitting up, wrapping his arms around his knees.

Quincy pulled his pajamas from the closet, a sense of dread suddenly coming over him. "Oh no, I forgot about school tomorrow. I am not excited, and you should not be either! School is a dreadful, awful place where bigger kids bully you, and the teachers despise you because of who your parents are. You do not know anything, Henry. You haven't even been there yet." He threw himself onto his bed, not bothering to cover up with the wool blanket.

"Miss. Nimms says that school is a good place. A good place to learn about all kinds of things, even stuff about other countries!"

Quincy loved his younger brother. He was the only friend he had ever had, but it was sad to see how little he knew about the world. "Miss. Nimms is a maid, Henry. What does she know about school?"

Henry didn't respond.

Quincy lay in bed that night, finally having to pull the covers over his shivering body. Such a large house was difficult to keep warm, especially upstairs. He had put school so far in the back of his mind that he had completely forgotten that he would be returning tomorrow.

"Why can't you teach us here? Why can't we be home-schooled like most of the other kids?" Quincy pleaded with his mother on the first day of winter break.

Beatrice made a face like she had just sat on a rabid raccoon, turning quickly to stare down at her oldest son. "Home-school? How would I look if I home-schooled my children? I would look just like one of those women from town, the ones who still walk to the market! I would not be caught dead doing the job of some teacher who can hardly afford to rent a room in that crummy boarding house at the edge of town. Please, Quincy, do not ask questions like that anymore. It's not nice."

School was another word for hell in young Quincy's mind; a never-ending nightmare that he could not wake himself up from. Maybe things would be better. Maybe Edward Cooper would be home-schooled this year. The name alone sent a chill down Quincy's spine, a chill that even the thick wool blanket could not warm.

Edward Cooper was a foot taller than Quincy, and much Broader, making him look like a grown man in a classroom full of children. "Your daddy going to save you when I bust open your stupid looking face? I bet you have never been in a fight. You're a little rich boy wimp!" Edawrd would shout on the playground, making the other kids in class stop what they were doing to take notice. "Are you going to call daddy? Is your daddy going to fire my daddy? Oh wait, he already did that!" Edward punched Quincy straight in the nose, knocking him on his back.

Crying for help was a waste of good breath. Mrs. Harel secretly watched from the schoolhouse window, rooting for Edward to do his worst to the oldest son of the man who had laid off her husband.

Quincy didn't sleep that night, he just stared out the window at the moon as it cast shadows in the deep white snow.

Chapter 2
Lessons learned In The Cold
(Quincy Shoultz)

The ride to school was terrible. The frigid air whistled through the slightly cracked front window. My mother blew the smoke from her cigarette through it before cracking the handle to roll it back up. The leftover smoke floated to the roof of the old car, making Henry and I lightheaded. "I don't want any trouble today in school, do you hear me?"

Henry and I nodded our heads, swiping furiously at the smoke cloud that danced in front of our faces. "Why are you dressed so nicely, mother? Are you going somewhere after you drop Henry and I off at the schoolhouse?"

My mother did not answer, she just glanced up, checking her red lipstick in the mirror as the Roadster plowed through the heavy mounds of snow.

"Your mother has a meeting at the bank with Mr. Garet. It's grownup stuff that you need not worry about." More often than not, my mother dismissed any inquiries from

Henry and I, brushing them off as silly children's questions.

I stared out the window at the never-ending plains of snow and dead trees. I always liked winter. The animals hibernating, the thick blanket of snow covering the tall grass that would normally sway in the breeze during the sweltering summer days. In the winter, time seemed to stand still.

Buildings began taking the place of the empty fields the closer we got to town. Most of the stores at the edge of town had old boards placed over the doors and windows, out of business signs pattered against them in the cold breeze. Butcher shops, tailors, restaurants, all closed years ago. I knew the mines had something to do with the town's downfall, therefore, my father was the first one to have angry fingers pointed in his direction. I slumped low in my seat, embarrassed that my mother decided to drive the newer of my father's cars to drop Henry and I off.

If it was not obvious by this point, my family was the richest family in all Obscurus, maybe even the state of Pennsylvania. To most, the dream of having multiple fireplaces in multiple rooms of their homes was a dream that would only ever be *that,* a dream. Most of the residents of Obscurus could hardly afford food for the week, living off a rotted head of cabbage boiled in hot water over an old woodstove.

"Those people look up to us. If they had worked as hard as your father when he was younger, they may be in a better place in life." My mother would say anytime I asked about the people in rags that gathered around a burning barrel in the alley by the old movie theater. I believed my mother for a while, believing that my father had just gotten lucky early on in his life, that maybe the towns folk were only bitter, jealous of my father's success.

"Look, it's the son of a heartless bastard!" The kids at school would shout relentlessly. The adult bystanders turned their heads, whispering to one another. "Do we *have* to go to school in town, mother? Henry and I do not fit in with the other kids, and its such a long drive to get us there."

My mother checked her face again in the mirror, she turned her head to the left, then to the right. "You will go to school with the other kids Quincy. *That* is final. We need to look like members of this community. Now more than ever. Besides, your father and I would have to send you far away for a private school education. You don't want to move far away from your family, do you?" Before I had a moment to respond, the car came to a sudden stop. "I'll be back in a couple of hours to pick you boys up. Behave, and listen to your teachers!"

It was pointless trying to reason with my mother. My voice was nowhere near as commanding as my father's.

My class consisted of nine other children my age. We crammed into the small schoolhouse by the old cemetery as soon as the morning church bells began to ring. "Do not let anything they say bother you. The school day only lasts for a few hours. We will be back home before you know it." I patted Henry on the back before he crossed the street with the children his age.

Henry's school was about a block and a half away. His teacher walked Henry and the rest of his class to their building from ours every school day. It was always sad watching my little brother being led away. It was even sadder knowing I would not be there to protect him.

"Get to class, rich boy!" Edward rammed his shoulder into mine, causing me to drop the schoolbooks I had wrapped in a leather belt loop. He laughed as he high fived another kid named Robbie Myer.

"What assholes." I scoffed, picking my books out of the snow.

"Welcome back everyone! Please take your seats so that we can begin today's lesson." Mrs. Harel stared at me for a moment; her eyes were empty, and as cold as the chill up my spine.

After a few hours of writing lessons, then math, it was time for recess, the most dreaded part of any school day for me.

"Well, well, look what we have here. It looks like the little rich boy and his pansy brother got dropped off in style today!"

Edward's voice crawled on my skin, stunning me like a venomous snake bite. I wanted to turn around, I wanted to confront this bully for the last time, I was just too afraid to do so. "What the matter, Shoultz? Daddy not here to buy you out of a pounding? How about *your* daddy hire *my* daddy back on at the mine, which *might* save you a world of hurt."

Edward and Robbie circled me like a pair of hungry hyenas, their mouths dripping with saliva, their claws scrapping the ground in front of them. "Yeah, tell your daddy that mine needs *his* job back as well!" Robbie hissed, his curly blonde hair like a flashlight in the daytime.

"Look, I don't want any trouble. I don't have anything to do with what my father does at the mines. I am just here to go to school, just like the two of you." I amazed myself, being able to muster full sentences in a time like this.

"Did you hear that, Robbie? Little rich boy thinks he is like us. He thinks we are all the same. Hey, Robbie, do you want to ride home to our big mansions that sit miles away from town? Do you want our mommies to come pick us up in big fancy yellow cars?"

Robbie laughed, not realizing that Edward *was not*. "My mother died last year of tuberculosis, just like most of the other people in this godforsaken town that your family looks down on from their castle on the hill."

Robbie cleared his throat, obviously feeling foolish for laughing. "I bet none of your family got sick. Did they, rich boy? I bet you all sat at a big table and ate goose with a heaping side of sweet potatoes, didn't you?"

I didn't know how to respond to Edward as he continued circling me, the rest of my class now dead silent. "Your father buried this town when he laid off all those workers. The sad part is, he didn't even have a damn reason to do so!"

I was suddenly pushed hard from behind, falling face first into Edward's chest. I was quickly grabbed up by the hood of my coat, Edward's face only inches from my own.

"Leave him alone!" a voice called out.

Edward turned to see Lana Kingsly, a girl from our class, standing with her hands on her hips, a disapproving look on her face.

"Let us head inside, children. That means *all* of you."

Edward turned to look at Mrs. Harel, her eyes fixated on the three of us. He turned back to me, his breath in the freezing air looked like a dragon who had just breathed fire. "This is *far* from over!"

I nodded my head, contemplating hitting Edward in the nose the second he released me. But of course, I did not. I never understood why my parents stayed in this place. Why would you want to live in a place where the few remaining residents hated your very existence? Maybe it had to do with the simple fact that my mother and father never had to spend more than ten minutes conversing with people who despised them; not like Henry and I did.

"These people. I'll never understand them." I would hear my father in his office, the smell of scotch and cigar smoke filling the air, soaking into the wood floors. "When things are running smoothly, they throw parades in my honor. When there is even the slightest hiccup, I am suddenly, the antichrist. There is no pleasing these people." I pictured my father's visitors nodding their heads in unison. "Those people can be replaced by more people. We will put some money towards fixing up the town. Bring in interested buyers, push out those who are not prone to adapting."

The group of men mumbled, taking sips of their drinks. "My father before me, his father before him, all great businesspeople, knew everything there was to know about running the mine. My father once dressed like the average worker before taking the elevator down and working side by side with his employees, you see? They respected him, believed every word out of his mouth. Now, there is all this talk of unionizing, fairness, higher wages, whispers amongst the men about a mass walkout. What has the world become when a man cannot even run his business without looking over his shoulder?"

I pulled my ear from the cold wooden door when I heard my mother coming up the steps behind me. "Quincy? What are you doing by your father's office door? He has particularly important company. You must not be a nuisance!" My mother placed her hand on the flat of my back, pushing me towards the stairs.

"I wasn't going to bother him. I was just walking by." I protested.

My mother acted as if she wasn't listening. "Miss. Nimms will have lunch ready soon."

I huffed loudly. Finally, my mother heard something that came from my mouth. "Do not huff, little man. Your father has a lot on his plate right now. No time for rambunctious children."

As well behaved as Henry and I were, you could see fit to forgive someone for forgetting that we were even still in the house. My mother did not see it that way. My mother saw Henry and I's very existence as a loud, obnoxious distraction to any and all adult activity, or conversation.

"Miss. Nimms?" I asked, as Henry and I took our places at the table for lunch.

Miss. Nimms rushed around us like her shoes were on fire. "What is it, Quincy? Miss. Nimms is in a hurry, *gotta* get this lunch out before your mother comes back down."

Henry smiled at me from across the table. I smiled back with a much *bigger* smile, creating a friendly competition as to who could smile the biggest. "What is it you needed?" Miss Nimms asked, finally able to take a deep breath. She was an older, colored lady, specks of gray glistened like silver in her pitch-black hair; her face worn and tired.

"Do the people in town hate my father?"

She looked around the room, checking for either of my parents who might be close by, then turned back to Henry and me. "People do not *hate* your daddy. They just don't understand the tough decisions he has to make. Don't take nothing those people down there say personally. They don't mean nothing by it. They just scared is all."

I stuck my fork into the slice of turkey on my plate, then looked back up at Miss. Nimms. "Is my daddy going to layoff all those people at the old mine when he starts up that new one a town over?"

Miss. Nimms looked around the room once more, before leaning forward in her chair. "I don't know anything about all that, honey. You just sit there and eat your lunch, no sense a boy your age worrying about all that grown-up non-sense."

My mother cleared her throat, making her presence in the room known. Miss. Nimms shot up from her chair, grabbing the dish rag she kept in her apron pocket. "Sorry, Mrs. Shoultz, just getting the boys here their lunch." Miss. Nimms started wiping down the spot where her arms had rested on the table.

"Thank you, Miss. Nimms, for that advice you gave *my* son. Here I was assuming you were just our housekeeper, now it has come to my attention that you are *also* the mother of my children."

Miss. Nimms bowed her head. "I'm sorry, madam. I didn't mean anything by it. It wasn't my place."

My mother smiled, then took her seat at the far end of the giant table. "That is correct, it is not your place. Your place is in the kitchen, the vicinity of a dirty clothes basket, and your room in the attic, not standing in the dining room spewing nonsensical gibberish to young children who do not understand the way of the world. Do I make myself clear?"

The room was silent, so silent you could hear the snowflakes tapping the window from outside. "I'm sorry, madam. It won't happen again." My mother waved her hand. Miss. Nimms nodded, then left the room.

"The audacity of that woman. It is painfully clear that she does not have children of her own. If she did, she would understand my frustration." I dropped my fork onto the plate, the piece of turkey still attached.

"Miss. Nimms was not doing anything wrong, mother. She was only speaking to us, not handing out life lessons on your behalf!" My tone was angry, but my mother hardly batted an eye.

"You and your brother are children. You do not have a say in this house. When you are old enough to contribute to the family name, then you may say and do as you please. Do you understand?" My mother shot at stern look in my direction, her eyes fierce, her lips pursed tightly, she then turned away; shaking her head as she pressed down on the wrinkled napkin in front of her.

"What do *you* contribute?" I asked, instantly regretting my choice of words. I heard Henry mumble something from across the table, his mouth too full of turkey for me to have understood what he was saying at that moment.

"What did you say to me?" I didn't have to look over to know that my mother's eyes were burrowing into me like a hungry owl watching a helpless field mouse. "Look at me!" my mother demanded, slapping her palms down on the table, causing Henry to spit out his mouthful of turkey. I slowly looked up, my eyes meeting my mother's.

I found myself without my lunch, sitting out in the snow, no jacket to keep me warm. "You can sit out there until you are ready to appreciate the life your father and I have given you. If you are so curious about those town people, you can live like them for a little while."

My mother slammed the front door shut. I nodded at Henry as he waved at me from the dining room window. I stood out in the cold for what felt like hours, burring my face in my lap as I cuddled up inside the small shed beside the house. I learned a valuable lesson on that day, I am just not sure what it was.

"Did you boys behave well in school?" my mother asked as Henry and I climbed into the back seat of the Roadster. There were two large white sacks stuffed in the floorboard at our feet, I wondered if they were sacks of laundry. I guess my mother had not noticed Henry's swollen lip, the swollen lip he did not have a few hours ago when she dropped us off for school.

"Are you alright, Henry?" I asked my little brother, taking his hand in mine.

Chapter 3
A Shoultz Family Curse
(Beatrice Shoultz)

I HATED DRIVING IN the snow, especially after the winter we have had thus far. I glanced into the rearview mirror, making sure my new lipstick was not smeared or cracking. The wintry weather dried my lips out the very second I opened the front door. Before looking back at the barely visible road, I glanced at my oldest son, Quincy. What an outspoken, brave little boy he was, even when *I* was at my worst. I knew both of my sons believed me to be overbearing, and even a bit harsh. But I had to be, I had to make sure that they grew up tough. If I had learned anything from watching my husband, you had to have thick skin if you wanted to survive in this world, especially *ours*. If being tough on my boys made them despise me, then so be it. At least they would grow to be resilient.

Both Quincy and Henry were exceptionally smart for their ages, so smart that Quincy had already mastered the piano we kept in the family room at home. We once invited a few of Alan's acquaintances over for dinner. They listened to Quincy play Chopin like it was second nature. And Henry, my sweet little boy, he was so well spoken, such a tremendous writer for someone so new to this world.

The car rattled as I drove over a large mound of snow. The boys bounced in the backseat, laughing at one another. This fancy new car did not seem designed to manage harsh winters, it would most likely need body work once we could get it to a decent enough mechanic. I am sure it seemed odd to the folks in town, seeing the lady of the house driving the car when we had a perfectly capable maid.

"I do not want that woman behind the wheel of *any* of our cars. We have worked too hard for them. The last thing I want is to find one wrapped around a tree on the edge of town. I will take the boys to school, and I will run the errands." I protested.

My husband shrugged his shoulders, taking a puff from his cigar. Since then, I was the only one driving to and from town.

"You boys better behave today!" I dropped Henry and Quincy off outside of the schoolhouse, ignoring the rude looks from the other parents who had just *walked* two and a half miles in the cold. I worried about the boys, even more so that they did not attend school in the same building. I had heard Quincy talking to Henry one night in Henry's room about standing up for himself, about not taking any crap off anyone at school. Was it *that* bad? Was life outside of the home a struggle for my boys? I did not like the thought of some dirty townie boy picking on either of my sons, it made me plain sick. Did they know who my husband was? Did they know their fathers could be jobless at the snap of Alan's fingers? I guess it didn't matter, considering most of the men in town had already been laid off anyway. It was a hiccup, that is all. Alan would figure it out, he would have everyone back in the mines working in no time, they just had to believe in him the way that I did.

I checked my makeup in the mirror one last time before glancing up at the old clock tower, not realizing what time it was. "Shoot!" I pressed the gas pedal to the floor; the wheels spun in the snow for a second before the Roadster shot forward. I had to get to the bank. I had to make sure that our money was still in good order. As soon as I approached Obscurus savings and loans, a security guard unlocked the door from the inside. He smiled and nodded.

"Good morning to you, Mrs. Shoultz!" Mr. Garet, the bank manager, extended his arm, softly pushing on my lower back.

Mr. Garet was a short, chubby man, wearing an *always* obvious toupee. "Right this way to my office." He choked out before coughing loudly. He pulled the handkerchief from his back pocket, wiping the spit from his lips.

"I do not plan to stay long, Mr. Garet. I have much to do today, and little time to do it." I sat down in the wooden chair in front of Mr. Garet's desk. He squeezed past me, his chubby belly brushing against my shoulders.

"Of course, madam, of course! What can I do for you today? When you phoned yesterday, you said something about needing to see the balance of your account with us." I placed my handbag on my lap, nodding my head. Mr. Garet smiled, his rosy cheeks smushing against the bottoms of his eyelids. "I checked on your account just a few moments before you came through the door. I am sure you will be quite pleased."

He slid a piece of paper across his desk, a number scribbled in pencil written on the top. "One would assume that my husband's money is the only thing keeping this establishments in business, otherwise you wouldn't have a guard unlocking the door before someone enters." I turned to look at the guard who had unlocked the door for me. "I'm glad you see the need to take extra security measures, especially considering the amount of money in the banks safe." I waved the little piece of paper around, just to remind Mr. Garet.

"There is a small, minor topic we need to discus here today." Mr. Garet folded his hands in front of him on his desk, beads of sweat dripping from his thick brow.

I stuffed the piece of paper into my handbag before crossing my legs and sitting straighter in the uncomfortable chair. I noticed some wrinkles in the blue dress tie that hung down in his lap. I wanted so badly to press them out. "What topic would that be, Mr. Garet? Would it be the topic of sharing my family's wealth amongst the town? You and the mayor would like a new courthouse, a new school so that all the children can attend together under one roof, open a few stores, giving jobs to those who do not wish to work in the mines. Does all that cover it, Mr. Garet?"

He cleared his throat, then shifted in his chair. "Um, well, yes. It would do this town some good if your family were to use your good fortune to polish up the town a bit. It sure would go a long way with the community." More beads of sweat dripped slowly down the chubby bank manager's face. "I know that you and Mr. Shoultz pay me quite handsomely to keep this bank up and running, keeping all that money safe and secure, but wouldn't it feel nice to help out your community, even just a little here and there?"

I wanted so badly to laugh in his face. The audacity of this man was unbecoming, and dare I say patronizing.

"Unbelievable. It truly is unbelievable." Mr. Garet looked on, slightly confused by my comment. "These people want my family's help to rebuild this town, the town that they themselves picked clean like the hungry vultures that they are. I am appalled. I am appalled that the people who do nothing but give me dirty looks every single time I drive into town, the people whose children pick on *my* children. They suddenly want help from us? That is laughable, Mr. Garet. Plain laughable. Where was the support from these people when my husband had to close the old mine? Where were these *needy* people when my daughter disappeared? Did they come to give my husband and I the love and support we needed in the worst of times? The answer is no, Mr. Garet." The bank manger's jaw dropped, he leaned back in his chair, seemingly perplexed. "Just for that, just for causing *me* such distress this morning, I would like to go ahead and withdraw every cent my family has in establishment. In other words, Mr. Garet, find yourself another job!"

I stood up from my chair. Mr. Garet's pudgy gut bumped against his desk as his heart rate increased. "Please, Mrs. Shoultz, forgive me. I didn't mean anything by it, please, reconsider!" He followed me into the small front lobby. The security guard's head shot up from the nap he had been taking.

I tucked the two large sacks of money into the backseat floorboard of the yellow Roadster. I looked up to see Mr. Garet staring through the bank window, his entire face now as red as his rosy cheeks. The security guard walked out, throwing his navy-blue uniform jacket to the sidewalk below. I turned away, hearing Mr. Garet shouting profanities at the top of his lungs through the bank window.

As I drove down the snow-covered street, I wondered if I had made a huge mistake, letting my emotions get the better of me. I wondered what Alan would think about this when *he* heard. I parked the car next to the old theater, remembering coming here years ago on Alan and I's first date. It felt like a lifetime had passed since then.

I shut the engine off, pulling my fur coat into my lap to keep my legs warm. I had about two hours before I had to pick the boys up from school. Nothing to do now but kill time. I considered driving back home, but driving all the way back to town would be miserable, especially in this snow.

Do we need anything at home? I wondered aloud, remembering I had just made a trip to the market in Prosper only two days ago. I tucked my arms under the thick fur coat, resting my face on the cold window. I drifted off into a dream that I had already had many times before.

"Mommy, can I play outside?" I glanced up from the blueprints that Alan and I were looking over for the new house.

"Yes darling, just don't wander too far. We don't quite know the area all that well and there could be sinkholes." I watched Susana scurry off out the through the unfinished front door frame. Her long blonde hair swaying back and forth as she skipped, her little white dress made her look like a little princess leaving her new castle to go on a morning stroll.

"Do you think she'll be alright playing on her own?" I asked Alan, who had not heard a single word.

"I think we should do a swinging door from the kitchen to the dining room, which would make it much easier for the staff to move freely from one room to another." Alan held up the blueprint, walking with it held up to his face like it was a map that held the secret location of buried treasure. "I will leave a note for the builders. They have done excellent work so far, don't you agree? Charles should be arriving soon with some important documents that need my signature. Be a dear and keep an eye out for him."

Alan lowered the blueprints, walking out of the room before I could answer. I moved a large sack of nails from the top of an old milk crate sitting in what was soon to be our family room. I sat upon it, crossing my legs, staring out into the fields of tall grass that stretched as far as the eye could see. An old silo caught my attention, it stuck out over the rolling hills, standing like a cloud gazing giant amongst the surrounding trees.

"Alan?" I called out to my husband, who had just re-entered the room, a large cigar in between his pointer and index fingers.

"Yes, dear?" he answered, eyes wide like he had forgotten that I was even still here.

"Do you think this is a wise choice, moving out here so far from town? It feels as if we are intentionally isolating ourselves from those people. I mean, they are your employees, and loyal employees at that. The fact that they decided to *trust* you and not unionize, trusting your words when you claimed that you would take care of them no matter what, that you would always be there. It just seems that moving all the way out here-"

Alan put his hand up and lowered his head, waiting for me to stop speaking. "My dear, those people live their own lives outside of the mines, same as I. When I said those things, I meant that I would look after their jobs, their wellbeing's at *work*. I cannot be there every minute of their lives, holding their hands, comforting and reassuring them. It would seem childish for my employees to hold ill-will towards moving my family a few miles outside of the town we have spent our lives in."

The moment that my husband uttered the words *family* and *childish*, I remembered my own child, the daughter I had not heard from since she last walked out through the front door.

"Susanna!" I called out, my heart racing, my palms sweating. I ran towards the front door, looking out into the vast, open field in front of the unfinished mansion. "Susanna!" I called out once more, still only hearing sounds of birds chirping in the distance.

"Do you see her?!" Alan ran out on the porch in front of me, panting loudly, his head turning nervously in every direction. "Susanna!" My husband shouted at the top of his lungs, so loudly that a flock of birds shot out from a tree near the gravel road. "Stay here, just in case she comes back while I'm gone!" Alan commanded, the veins pulsating in his neck.

My husband ran off around the house. I had never seen him run so quickly. I sat down on the top step of the unpainted porch, praying to God that Alan would find my little girl. Just as I looked up towards the heavens, I heard the father of my only child screaming. I knew at that moment my prayers would not be answered.

"Susanna!" I screamed, dropping my fur coat to the wet floorboard below. No matter the number of times I have experienced that reoccurring nightmare, it never gets easier to calm myself after.

Chapter 4
The Value Of Copper
(Edward Copper)

"Little brat. He thinks he can walk away without facing the consequences? He is dead freaking wrong!"

The cold stung my face, more so than usual. My walk home took thirty-five minutes, give or take, all depending on how many times I would have to stop and retie my boots or kick a mound of snow from my path. I thought about today at school, that little rich boy pansy, thinks he is better than me because he gets to ride in a car to school, chauffeur driven by his mommy. I would show him. I would show him that people in this town are not going to stand for it any longer. I passed by some of the old department stores, then up past the train tracks, then up through the woods until I reached home.

Obscurus was a dead town, even deader in the winter. Everyone stayed inside, all huddled together around their wood burning stoves, fighting to stay warm on the harder to manage days. Pa had me outside for hours last week cutting up wood for our stove. I nearly passed out after stacking it all neatly against the back of the outhouse. If not for that stove, me, my sister Emily, and my paw, we would freeze to death. Our house was not the worst place to call home in Obscurus. I had seen worse places that some of my classmates walked home to after school, places that made me plenty thankful for what *we* had.

"Eddie, you home from school? If so, fetch some water down by the creek, gonna need it for super if you wanna eat tonight." Pa called out from the back bedroom.

My kid sister, Emily, sat on the floor in the living room, coloring on a piece of paper she must have taken from school.

"You alright, Em?" I asked, peaking my head around the corner. Emily looked up at me with a smile, showing the gaps where two of her baby teeth had fallen out.

"Go and get that water. Don't be wasting time!" Pa called out, coughing up a lung in the process.

Pa was not originally from Pennsylvania. He moved up here from Tennessee back in 1919 or 1920, I cannot remember which. A friend of his talked him into it, convinced him there was money to be made up north. From the stories Mama told me before she passed, Pa's friend ended up getting real sick; died of pneumonia or something like that. Pa ended up working for Mr. Shoultz in the coal mines, a job he always looked down on in his younger days.

Mama always said that Pa had big dreams of owning his own restaurant somewhere in town. I guess after his friend died, Pa lost all that motivation. I guess he lost even more once Mama got sick and he was laid off from working in the mines. I grabbed hold of the bucket from outside by the collapsed shed, then headed down the hill towards the creek. "Guess it's cabbage again tonight." I sighed, filling the bucket as high as I could after breaking the thin layer of ice with the heel of my boot. It felt like this snow was not ever going to melt, just seemed it was going to keep coming down until it buried this godforsaken town alive.

I made it back up the hill, most of the water still in the bucket. The rest ran down my pants leg and into the side of my untied boot.

"You couldn't get any more?" Pa asked, taking the bucket from my hand once I stepped inside.

"Sorry, Pa. Most of it ended up on my pants. Getting up the hill is a nightmare. I almost-"

Pa slammed the bucket on the kitchen counter, causing it to splash up into his thick brown beard. "Then you go and get more, boy. How hard is it to go and fetch water? Good thing I didn't send you out to hunt for rabbits or squirrels. Who in the hell knows if we would ever eat again."

I bowed my head in shame. "Sorry, Pa. I'll head back down and grab some more." I reached for the bucket handle, only to be swatted away.

"Just go and sit with your sister. I don't like that she has to be by herself so much."

The pain in Pa's voice was the only thing that kept me from lashing out after working so hard only to be yelled out for not doing the task to *his* liking. I knew how much Pa hurt; I knew how hard it had been on him since he lost Mama. I just wished that he understood that he was not the only one who lost her. I wish he realized that Emily and I were hurting just as badly.

"Hey, Em. What are you drawing?" I asked, sitting down on the floor next to her. She lifted the picture she had drawn with a broken pencil; I assumed it was of *her* and another kid from school. "Is that you and a friend?" I asked curiously, taking the picture in my hand.

"Yeah, it is me and Henry Schoultz, my friend from school. I drew this picture for him because I feel bad that he got hit in the face today by this mean kid named Hershel." I gritted my teeth. The thought of my little sister being friends with *any* member of that family made my blood boil.

"You do not have to feel sorry for that kid, Em. No one in this town should feel sorry for them. They live in a mansion miles away, they eat oven roasted bird and freshly baked bread for dinner that a housekeeper makes for them. They also drink water from their sink, not from a dirty bucket *I* filled in a creek." Emily stared up at me, her little green eyes filled with sadness and confusion.

"You are too young to remember, but that boy's daddy laid off Pa when Mama was real, real sick. That family is the reason Pa could not afford a doctor from out of town to come and help Mama. That family hoards away all their money in that bank, lording it over all our heads as we freeze and starve to death. Do you understand?"

It was obvious that Emily did not understand. She was just a little girl who did not know any better.

"I'm sorry, Em. You be friends with whomever you want. This is a beautiful drawing." Emily smiled as I patted her on the head.

"Supper is ready! You two get in here and eat." Pa called out from the kitchen.

The smell of boiled cabbage filled the house. We all sat down at the table, holding hands to say grace. "Emily, you can lead us in prayer tonight, darlin." Pa did his best to force a smile at Emily. The sadness on his face was a permanent reminder of what had been taken from us too early.

"God bless this food and those who are about to receive it. Thank you for my big brother, Edward, Pa, and Mama, I hope she is an angel by your side. In your name we pray, amen."

I could tell Pa was impressed with Emily. His smile towards her felt almost genuine.

"That was beautiful, darlin. Your mama would be proud. I just wish she were sittin' here with us now." Pa lowered his head, fighting back tears. He was never one to wear his emotions on his sleeve, always held it all in, even in front of Emily and I.

"Mama might still be here if it wasn't for that rich, greedy, son of a-"

Pa slapped the table, rattling our bowls of cabbage soup, scaring Emily. "Just stop with all the bad mouthin'. Ain't no need for it, especially at the dinner table. Your mama would not want you speakin' that way about anybody. Now, it was not Mr. Shoutz's fault we got laid off, it has a whole bunch to do with the economy, stuff you would not understand." Pa patted Emily on the back, then kissed her on the head before grabbing his bowl of cabbage soup and heading towards the couch in the living room. He coughed loudly before making it there, spilling some of his soup on the rug. "Damn cough has got me up all night, can't hardly breathe."

Pa sat down on the couch, drinking his soup from the bowl like it was the last drop of water in the hottest of deserts. Though Pa would never admit it. Even sitting on the very edge of death, he would never admit that he was sick. It was not the same kind of sickness that mama had, but like tuberculosis, it was a sickness of the lungs. "Look at what they did to us!" I shouted, even surprising myself.

Pa looked up from his bowl, catching cabbage juice with his beard.

"Those bastards have taken everything from us! We didn't have the money to help Mama because they laid you off, we are on the brink of foreclosure. I saw the papers they left on the front door! Now, look at you!" I stood up from the table, feeling like I went from child to adult man within seconds. "You spend all day and night coughing. I've seen the blood on your pillows. Do you know what that means, Pa? That means you have black lung disease from being down in those *damned* mines for all those years! The Shoultz family has run everyone worth anything out of town. They are evil people who do not care at all about the folks they have hurt." I was out of breath by the time I finished shouting. Pa and Emily just stared at me like I had finally lost my mind.

Pa sat his bowl down on the floor beside the couch before placing his hands firmly on his knees. "Your mama coughed up blood too. Hers was due to tuberculosis. How do you know I don't have the same thing? You are so quick to put all this blame on Mr. Shoultz and his family. It was *me* who made the choice to go down in those mines. I knew the risks; we all knew the risks. I needed a job and Mr. Shoultz was hirin'. Nobody *forced* me to work, Edward! I am sorry, I tried my hardest to be a good daddy to you and your sister, I really did. I hope you will find it in your hearts to forgive me when my time draws near. I just- I just wish I could have been something that you two kids could be proud of." Pa lowered his head. Tears dripped down onto his shirt. Emily and I ran over, wrapping our arms around our father as he cried louder than any of us ever had.

As time moved forward and the cold snow packed itself under ever colder snow, Emily and I watched as Pa grew sicker and sicker. On Tuesday, December 23rd, 1932, my father passed away. Emily and I hopped on a train just two towns over, headed down to Tennessee to live with our great aunt Debra. I cannot say that I will miss the small coal mining town of Obscurus, or the few friends I made in my time there. But there is one thing I did before leaving, something that will stick with me until the day I am laying warm in my bed, surrounded by ten grandkids, my hand being held by someone who loved me. I will never forget the day I made amends with Quincy Shoultz.

Chapter 5
All the Time In the World
(Dean and Jeffery)

Time passed differently in Obscurus, according to who you asked. Some folks say that during the winter it felt as if Obscurus sat still, not moving even to brush the extra layer of snow from its frozen back. The rest of the world went on its way, never glancing back to take a final look at the dreary little mining town.

Thomas Downs knew this firsthand, more so than most of the other residents. Thomas sat in the alley behind what was once his feed store. "Stop on by Downs feed store. We have everything your farm needs!" he would say on the street corner, smiling, happy, unaware of the harsh, unforgiving future that lay ahead. At least the fire in the old, rusted oil drum kept him warm during the cold nights.

"Going to be another cold one tonight, I can feel it in my bones." Thomas commented as Georgina brought a buddle of old newspapers next to where the barrel sat. Georgina had worked at the animal clinic just a few blocks away, all the way up until it closed its doors for the final time.

"You say that all the time, you thick-headed old fool! Why can't your old bones say anything else? Every night is cold, has not been a warm night since early October."

Georgina was a few years younger than Thomas, but liked to joke that he was old enough to be her great-grandfather. "Some nights are colder than others, you know that. I would pull the boards off that door if I could, huddle up on the floor of my store and sleep like a baby."

The old buildings owned by the bank looked like investments, if the right buyers ever came through town. The sight of a bunch of bums living in them would surely drive down the property value.

"Heck, go ahead and do it. Might get you a night in jail. At least you would have some place warm to sleep, and a bed. Oh, how I miss having a bed."

Georgina threw a stack of newspapers in the old barrel. The flash shot up, sending little embers floating around like fireflies, only to wither away once they landed in the thick white snow. "Naw, don't want anything on my record. I've had good standing in this town for the past thirty years. I don't want to sully that for anything, not even a warm bed." Thomas exclaimed, raising his old pointer finger in the air.

"You really think anyone cares about all that, Thomas? Do you really think there is anyone left with a shred of dignity in this frozen hell of ours? You must do what you can to survive out here. If not, this cold will eat you alive, right along with that *good standing* of yours."

Thomas shook his head and smiled. "I must keep whatever I have left as close as I can. I will not let these troubles strip them away from me like a thief in the night. There are still good people in this town, Georgina. They are all just buried under their own troubles. You can't fault anyone for that."

Georgina laughed, throwing another stack of papers in the fire. "What are you going on about, old man? I tell you, half of the time I don't even think *you* know what is coming out of that mouth of yours."

Thomas laid his head back, looking up at the gray sky. "Things will work out. Sometimes we must experience hardship. We cannot have clear skies all the time." Thomas closed his eyes and smiled a little, picturing his late wife shaking her head in frustration after he forgot to restock the shelves in the store.

"What am I going to do with you?" she would ask, laughing as she tossed him the broom, the same one she was using to sweep up piles of dirt a customer had brought in.

"There you go, drifting off into dream land again. Make sure you grab me a hot cup of coffee before you leave." Georgina laughed as Thomas Downs dozed off to sleep with a big smile on his face. He slept great that night, staying warm until it was time to wake up and start another day.

"How do I get fired from the only decent job left in this town?" Fredrick Newman asked himself, wishing he had not given back the security uniform he threw on the ground in a fit of rage.

"I just don't see the need for a security guard when there is nothing left to guard. Don't you see that?" The bank manager's voice played over and over in Fredrick's mind, frustrating him further.

"What am I going to tell Annie? She is going to be devastated." Fredrick stopped in the middle of the street, just a block away from the home he shared with his wife, Annie. "It wasn't something that *I* did. It was that miserable lady, Mrs. Shoultz."

Fredrick took a deep breath, then wrapped his arms around himself, trying anything to stay warm until he reached home. "Fredrick? Is that you? Why on earth are you home so early?"

Annie came from the kitchen, a damp dishcloth strewn over her left shoulder. Fredrick scratched his head, removing the uniform cap he forgot he was still wearing. "Well, honey, that's a good question."

Annie placed her hands on her hips. "Do not tell me that you lost your temper and got yourself fired. You are getting too old, Fredrick. Jobs are hard to come by these days. We are lucky to still have this house. You know, if not for that little bit of money your daddy left, we would be sleeping in an alley somewhere, burning trash in a barrel just to keep warm."

Fredrick put his hands up defensively, like he wanted to block his wife's words from slapping him in the face. "It was not my fault. I swear on it. Mrs. Shoultz took all her money out of the bank. Every last penny. The bank is not going to pay me to guard an empty safe. I told you, Annie, coming here was a mistake. We should have stayed with your brother until I found a job up there!"

Fredrick tossed his cap on the back of the sofa before plopping down on it. Annie still stood in the kitchen doorway with her hands on her hips. "We still have about nine-hundred-dollars left in the old hatbox. Let's take it and figure out what we're going to do. Can't sit around here waiting. Not at our age." Annie sighed, patting her husband on the head before heading into the kitchen to finish the dishes.

"Sorry, honey." Fredrick added, sticking his head over the back of the couch. Annie looked in with the smile that always brought him comfort when things didn't seem to be working in their favor.

"It's okay. It's certainly not the end of the world." Fredrick laid his head back on the couch, never feeling luckier in his life.

"Damn bus is always late, which in turn, makes us late." Jeffery moaned, kicking built up pile of snow next to the bus stop. Dean sighed, rolling his eyes after hearing the same complaint *every* morning.

"Come on, stop your moaning. I mean, it is not like we are getting in trouble over it. The boss knows that our bus route blows. He knows we are trying to get the hell out of this town and get closer to the mine."

Jeffery pretended to beat his head on the lamp post just a few feet away. "Yeah, we may not get in any trouble, but it certainly hurts our paychecks, smart guy!"

Dean knew that he did not have an argument. "Yeah, it does hurt the paycheck, but it will be smooth sailing once we get ourselves one of those townhouses that Mr. Shoultz owns. We just have to wait it out until a few other schmucks decide to call it quits, then it's ours."

Dean dreamed every night about him and his brother Jeffery moving into the newly built townhouses just a few miles from the new mines. The houses were designed for the mine workers, their wives, and a minimum of two children. "Can you imagine getting out of here and living in Prosper? That town has an actual market, clothing departments, nice restaurants... You name it, they have it."

Jeffery leaned his head against the cold bus window as it burrowed loudly through the snow and ice. He hung on every word that came from Dean's mouth. The thought of living in Prosper truly sounded like heaven. "I hear the committee is thinking about starting construction on a newer set of homes even closer to the mines. Heard they were going to be like tiny mansions." Jeffery smiled, excited to contribute to the beautiful portrait his brother had painted him.

Dean frowned, shaking his head and rolling his eyes. "Who on earth told you *that*?" Dean asked, turning Jeffery's cheeks red with embarrassment.

"I heard it from Keith, down in the mine yesterday on break. I swear it!" Jeffery tried avoiding eye contact, knowing his older brother could read him like a book. Dean showed mercy, acting excited about the rumor.

"That would be pretty swell little brother. Pretty damned swell." The welcome sign for Prosper appeared over the hills. Dean felt a whirlwind of excitement every time he saw it.

"What do you think will happen to Obscurus once Prosper is finished?" Jeffery asked, sitting up in the seat next to his brother.

"Heck, I don't know and really don't care. Good riddance if you ask me. Those sad sacks who still try to make something of that place will only get buried under it when they bulldoze the place." Dean remarked, a cheeky grin on his face. Jeffery did not find joy in the thought of their childhood home being crushed under the weight of some giant machine; all those memories being burned in huge bonfires stretching for miles.

"The way I see it, Mr. Shoultz and his shirt tucking cigar club will finally come to their senses and realize that Obscurus is a lost cause with nothing worth saving. I bet within a year, he and his family will have built themselves a huge mansion overlooking the Proser mines." Dean rubbed his hands together in excitement, the thought of making Prosper his permanent home was a dream that sat just barely out of arms reach.

"What happens if they do that draft thing that the government has been talking about on the radio? What if we get sent off to fight in some war?" Jeffery asked, feeling a nervousness come over him.

Dean huffed loudly, rolling his eyes once more. "That is just a fear tactic, little brother. "There is no way that the government is going to force anyone to put their lives on the line, especially fellow Americans like us." Dean's confidence always made Jeffery feel better.

Jeffery did not feel that nervous feeling in his gut again until two years later when America implemented the military draft of 1941. Jeffery received his letter in the mailbox of his and Deans townhouse they had just moved to. After learning that his older brother was not going with him, Jeffery took his own life shortly after. He was laid to rest in the Prosper County Cemetery. His brother Dean would join him ten-years later after a mining accident. Dean would be buried next to his little brother at the age of twenty-four.

Chapter 6

Without Labor, Nothing Prospers

(Harold Brey)

The days were short, and the nights grew colder in Obscurus as what little life remained scurried about to keep themselves warm. Strong, silent gusts of wind brushed the top layer of snow against the side of the old equipment shed by the mine entrance.

It was the day before Christmas Eve, the aroma of freshly brewed coffee and buttered toast circled the break area, the same way it did every morning at this time. Harold Brey tucked his hands into the pockets of his once brown coat that had since turned black from his time down in the mines. Harold covered his face as a gust of freezing wind passed by him, swirling around his frozen feet.

"Damn bus, always late, always a pain in the rear." Harold grunted, looking down the path in the road where the city bus came through to drop off the few workers still living in Obscurus. "They should just close the town for good, tell all those bums to quit whining about the old mine being shut down, get off their butts, and come put all that experience to work over here." Harold talked to himself to keep his throat from freezing up. He knew he would need every bit of his voice once the bus arrived with the rest of his crew.

"You out here talking to yourself again, Harold? You know, I wish I could execute a conversation with *myself* the way you do. I'd never get lonely." Kevin Taylor laughed, patting Harold on the shoulder before heading back over to the break area to make sure he was not burning the toast.

"This bus, it never fails to be late, you know?" Harold asked, throwing his hands up in frustration. "It is always my butt that gets a chewing out because of the lack of work getting done in *my* quadrant. I tell them, the bus being late is not my fault, they just give me that smug look." Harold had not noticed that Kevin was too far away by now to hear his complaining.

The sound of the bus engine roared over the far hill. Smoke rolled from the back, creating a giant black cloud that followed just a few feet behind. "Its about time!" Harold pulled his pocket watch from his coat, shaking his head at the time. "Thirty-minutes late. Simply perfect."

Harold jogged towards the bus as it pulled in the large parking area, the big black tires sliding in the snow as the bus came to a halt. The sound of the air brakes engaging let Harold know it was time to give the bus driver a good tongue-lashing. The doors opened like an accordion as the handful of Obscurus residents piled down the steps.

"Every day, every freaking day you are late getting these guys here! What is the problem? And how can we fix it? This is getting ridiculous!" Harold shouted, smacking the glass on the folded door.

The bus driver, a thin Black man threw his hands up, feeling his *own* form of frustration. "What am I supposed to do about the snow, huh? What do you want me to do about it? I should not even have to be picking these guys up anymore! Why are you still bussing in workers from Obscurus, Huh? Any reasoning for that? They can't be like the rest of the people down there, the ones who refuse to move up here to work after getting canned?"

The driver pulled the lever to close the doors before Harold could respond. He took a step back, watching the bus driver continue to make hand gestures towards him as he pulled away. "I am a colliery official, you schmuck! I do not have a say in where you have to pick workers up!"

Like Kevin Taylor before, the driver was too far away by now to hear Harold's complaints.

He turned to see the men already at the equipment shed pulling on their coveralls and tool belts. "Don't forget to check the light on your helmets *before* we go down! I don't want to be running back up here all day to get new ones!"

The men nodded, grabbing pickaxes from the rack.

"You two!" Harold called out, singling out Dean and his younger brother, Jeffery.

Harold never liked Jeffery, always thought he was too young and inexperienced to be down in the mines. "I want you two working today, not jabbering back and forth like a couple of schoolchildren. Do you hear me? I will send one of you to Dino's section if I have to get on you *once* today."

Dino was another colliery official that none of Harold's men liked, for reasons too long for any one man to list. Dean and Jeffery nodded their heads, grabbing their picks and shovels behind everyone else.

"You fellas going down soon?" a woman's voice called out from behind Harold. "Starting a bit late, aren't you? Most of your men have been down there for the past hour, give or take."

Harold rolled his eyes at the red headed woman in wearing the same coveralls as the rest of the workers. "The bus was late again, like all the other times. It's not something I can control." Harold had been a mine worker for the past ten years. He had even worked the mines in Obscurus before they closed. Unlike most of the workers from Obscurus, Harold did not rebel against the idea of having to move from his home to be closer to the mine in Prosper. He never quite understood how some of the best friends he had ever had could just drop to their knees and call it quits, refusing to move, hating Mr. Shoultz and his committee for the choices they made. He just liked to work hard, plain, and simple. He had moved his wife and six-year-old-daughter up here as soon as he caught wind about the Obscurus mine shutting down. He was glad that he made the choice to move and was offered an instant promotion for his willingness and dedication.

"Those excuses aren't going to fly when you have the big bosses breathing down your neck, wondering why your team has made the least amount of progress this year."

The woman giving Harold so much gripe was Felica Mcdowal, a hardnosed kick in the pants who was always ready to throw her co-workers under the bus at any given time. She was the third colliery official, no more a *big boss* than Harold or Dino, but liked to act like she ran it all. Harold would have found her attractive if not for her having the muscular build of a short man, and a permanent smug look on her freckled face.

He remembered seeing her at the market one Saturday morning without her filthy coveralls and a layer of coal dust on her face. He could not believe how normal she looked surrounded by the norm. He had planned to say hello, or maybe give her a nod in passing, but was surprised by what he saw. Just as Harold rounded the dry goods aisle, he noticed Felica standing rather close to another woman who looked to be a few years younger than her. The woman's hand rested flat oh Felica's lower back as she stroked her hand through Felicia's thick red curls.

Harold turned quickly, hoping they had not seen him. From then on out, he couldn't stop thinking about the situation he had almost interrupted.

"Excuses? Are you kidding, Felica? How am I supposed to control the bus, Huh? Please do explain if you have any ideas."

Harold turned away from Felica, heading onto the platform with his team. The steel platform creaked loudly, the cables holding the platform jerked from left to right, as the platform was lowered down into the darkness. "Who is she to talk to *me* like that? I have been here twice as long as she has. It's probably because she *thinks* she is going to be a manager. Well, she has another thing coming."

Harold's team side-eyed each other on the way down, laughing, mocking Harold behind his back as he mumbled angrily. The platform reached the bottom, stopping with a loud thud.

"Alright, listen up. I want Dalton and Nicholas feeding the bunker, Dean and Jeffery on vein duty. I want you two exactly where Nicholas and Dalton left off yesterday, not ten feet to the left of it. James, Marty, and Fransico, I want you three on carts. Let's try to have a good shift. I know you all ended up with the grunt work, but that is what happens when you're late every day." Harold clapped, making his team break off and head to their workplaces.

The only lights available were the headlamps, making it almost impossible to work safely. Over the years, Harold had seen his fair share of mine-related accidents. From guy's falling in sinkholes, to getting run over by full carts. He once saw a woman get cracked in the head with a piece of falling rock. Anyone who had spent time in the mines knew the risks involved during the workday, and even years after. He thought about a friend of his that he worked the mines with in Obscurus, a man named Thomas Copper. Copper stayed in Obscurus after the layoff, his wife had gotten really sick with tuberculosis before passing away in her sleep one night.

Harold wished he could have done something to help Thomas, especially with him having a son, and a young daughter to care for. But he had his own life, his own family to look after. He just wished things did not have to be the way they were sometimes.

He considered himself lucky; lucky to have a healthy little girl and a beautiful wife waiting for him once he climbed up and out of this blackened hellhole. Suddenly, just as Harold had drifted off into a daydream about the cornbread his wife would be cooking up for dinner that night, there was a loud crashing sound that erupted from tunnel three. Suddenly, everyone rushed towards it, headlamps bobbling up and down in the pitch-black chaos.

"What happened?" Harold heard Dino shout over the crowd that had formed around a large hoist at the end of tunnel three.

He pushed past the workers, making his way towards a collapsed hoisting arm, his heart racing, knowing what he was about to see would make him miss being safe at home even more.

"Felica!" Harold called out, scrambling to her side as she lay crumbled on the ground, a thick steel beam lying acrost her chest. "What happened?" he shouted at one of Felica's men.

The man was crying so hard that Harold couldn't make out a single word. The black coal dust on the worker's face mixed with the tears, making it look like beads of motor oil running down his cheeks.

"The- the- the beam snapped. Felica was standing next to me!" the man dropped to his knees, crying over the chatter in the background.

"Harold?" Harold glanced down into Felica's tear-soaked eyes, blood dripped from the corners of her lips and nose. He grabbed Felica's hand, squeezing it tightly in between his own.

"I'm here."

He leaned forward, Felica's voice was frail and weak, nothing like the strong, commanding voice that had screamed at him a hundred times over the past year and a half. "I'm really sorry. You know that, right?" Felica asked, trying to pull her head off the ground.

"Don't talk. Save your strength. Dino is up top getting help as we speak. We are going to get you out of here, I promise." Felicia forced a smile but knew damn well that the last light she would ever see was the dimly lit one on Harold's head.

"Do me a favor, would you?" Felica asked, her smile slowly fading. "Give my ring to Ashley. You tell her that I loved her more than I have ever loved anybody. You tell her that. You tell her for me."

Harold felt Felica's ring slip off her finger and into the palm of his hand. "It sucks, you know? You cannot ever hide from death. It finds you, even in the darkest places."

Her eyes slowly shut; the chatter of concerned voices trailed off down the tunnel. Harold placed the ring in his coat pocket, knowing that once Felica's body was removed from the mine, work would have to resume, like nothing had happened.

The platform reached the top. The sun had just started to set over the hills in the distance, the orange hue drenching the white blanket of snow for just a few moments before turning into a dark shadow over the land. The nighttime cold made it hurt to move your body; it made your brain plead for *any* amount of warmth it could find.

"Hell of a thing, huh?"

Harold turned around, forgetting the rest of his team had been on the platform with him. Dean and his brother Jeffery came to his side, patting him on the shoulder. "Yeah, hell of a thing, boys."

He reached into his coat pocket, running his pointer finger across the silver band. "I'm going to head over to Nick Scarbrough's tavern for a drink, then stop by- um, stop by Felica's place."

Dean and Jeffery had already made their way towards the city bus that would be taking them back to Obscurus. They didn't hear a word Harold had said. He lowered his head, watching as the deep footprints in the snow slowly started to fill in.

The engine roared to life in Harolds 1932 DeVaux 67-5 series, the first car he had ever bought and paid for. He sat for a moment, staring up at the coal bunker. A thick cloud of black smog floated up towards the heavens. He smiled, knowing Felica wouldn't mind.

After a few cold pints of Iron City beer, Harold sat in the corner of Scarbrough's tavern, staring down at the ring Felica had handed to him. "Of all people, my ugly mug had to be the last one you ever saw. Guess I'm sorry about that as well."

Nick Scarbrough side-eyed Harold as he restocked the shelves behind the bar with freshly dried mugs. Nick had seen Harold sitting in the corner booth around this time since the day he cut the ribbon on the front door, but they had never spoke more than a handful of words to one another.

Something seemed off about Harold tonight, something seemed to be weighing heavily on his mind. "You doing alight there, Bud? Can I get you anything else? Like always, try to keep a lid on the whole beer drinking thing. Can't have the law poking around with this whole prohibition thing going on."

Nick knew he didn't have to worry about any of his patrons blabbing about the beer. He had only hoped to brighten Harold's dim demeanor, if only just a little.

Nick poured himself a cup of coffee, taking a slow sip to avoid burning his tongue. Harold looked up, as if he had been in a trance the entire time, only to be snapped out of it by Nick's attempt at conversation. He took a moment to look back down at the ring, before slipping it back into his pocket.

"I'm good. Rough night, that's all," he answered with a half-smile before dropping four dollars on the table and sliding out from the corner both. He nodded with a smile, then walked back out into the cold, thinking about the last stop he had to make before heading home to his family.

Chapter 7
Such A Quiet Place To Sleep
(Miss Nimms)

I threw out what was left of dinner from the night before. It seemed like such waste. "Would you like me to run these leftovers into town, Mrs. Shoultz?" I asked, already knowing the answer before it passed through the lady of the house's lips.

"And how would you go about getting all that leftover food into town, Miss. Nimms?" I glanced down at all the uneaten quail, the bread, the green beans, all that I was about to toss out like garbage.

"I'll happily put it on a sled and drag it there, Madam." I kept a straight face, trying my hardest not to smile at the bewildered look on Mrs. Shoultz's face in that moment.

"Miss Nimms, I'm not sure if you're trying to be humorous, but I haven't the patience for it today." She rubbed her fingers on her temples, her eyes fixated on the opened book that young Quincy had left out on the side table next to the couch. She patted her gown, becoming increasingly frustrated the more she stared. "Those boys, they never learn to pick up after themselves."

Trivial things like that really seemed to bother Mr. Shoultz, even more so than the wrinkles she would find on the dresses in her wardrobe. "Is it too much to ask that they clean up? I don't think it's asking much, do you?" She asked after I had dumped the leftovers down by the woods, now dusting the overly expensive junk that sat on the mantel of the large fireplace.

"Not at all, Mrs. Shoultz. Not at all." I responded, feeling her eyes now on my back, watching every stroke I made with the duster.

"Take the items off the mantel first. You're certainly missing most of the dust just out of pure laziness."

I rolled my eyes, wishing I had not started dusting with the head of the household being present in the room.

I had worked for the Shoultz family for quite some time, considering myself lucky to still be employed at all. Mr. Shoultz had invited a bunch of his friends in the suits over, the next day half the town was out of work. I watched with my own two eyes as the place that I had grown so fond of faded away. Mr. Shoultz sat in his giant leather chair, staring out at the very place he had drained life from, puffing on his cigar, sipping on his scotch. There were other housekeepers who worked by my side during the downfall.

Other employees like me, who *also* felt the wrath of Mrs. Shoultz and her unsatiated need for perfection. They came and they went, until it was just *me* who catered to every need in the Shoultz household. It was not a backbreaking job; I had certainly had worse in my day.

After finishing the fireplace in a manner that Mrs. Shoultz found acceptable, I moved upstairs, passing by young Quincy's bedroom.

"Hello, Miss. Nimms!" he called out, looking up from something he was drawing, sitting at the row-top desk in the far corner.

"Hey there, Quincy. I see you are working just as hard as your daddy."

He smiled up at me as I stood beside him, glancing down at what he was so focused on. "Are you writing a letter to someone?" I asked curiously, trying to read the first few sentences, hoping It did not seem like I was prying.

He put down his pencil, reading slowly over the few paragraphs he had already written. "It's a letter to Edward Copper, a kid from school. Edward's father just passed away and I think that he is moving to Tennessee with his aunt."

I sat down at the foot of Quincy's bed, hoping Mrs. Shoutz had not followed me up the steps without my noticing. "Is this Edward a friend of yours?" I asked, setting down the bucket of cleaning supplies I had carried with me. Quincy functioned as if he were about to turn and answer but put his head down instead. "Is this that boy I hear you telling henry about? The same boy who calls you all those nasty names?"

Quincy nodded, still not wanting to look in my direction. "Well, it is mighty nice of you to write this boy a letter, especially after how he's treated you at school. You know, that makes you a pretty great person in my book." Quincy finally turned his head, just slightly looking over his shoulder. I could see the tears in his eyes.

These boys were nothing like their mama and daddy. Nothing at all. If anything, these boys were the embodiment of all the *good* that had been sucked out of this family years ago. I knew young Quincy was not made aware that he once had a sister, a sister that disappeared without a trace before he was even born. I had always wondered why Mr. and Mrs. Shoultz never told the boys about her, but I knew it was not my place to question their parenting.

"Sometimes, I don't feel like a good person, Miss. Nimms." Quincy whispered, wiping his nose with the sleeve of his shirt.

I stood up from the bed, walking over, and kneeling down at his side. "Why do you say that? You are one of the nicest people I have ever met, Quincy."

The boy wrapped his arms around my neck, crying even harder now. "So many people in town hate us, Miss Nimms. They hate my family. I don't want my family to be hated. I would give anything for everything to be normal, I really would! My little brother Henry does not deserve to be hated or talked badly about. He is a good boy, and he loves everyone no matter what they say or do!"

I wrapped my arms around Quincy in return, my heart feeling heavier and heavier the harder he cried. "What is wrong with my son?" Mrs. Shoutz asked, her hands firmly placed on her hips, her eyes piercing through me.

"I am sorry, Madam. It is just that Quincy was-"

Mrs. Shoultz put her hand up, letting out a deep breath before placing it back on her hip. "It is not your place to comfort my son I feel as if we've had this same discussion very recently. Would I be correct, Miss. Nimms?"

I stood up quickly, grabbing the handle of my cleaning bucket. "Excuse me, I would like that you answer my question." Mrs. Shoultz blocked the door with her body before I could get past. "What kind of example would I be setting for my son if I were to just let you go without an explanation as to why one of my employees feels the deep inclination to *keep* going behind my back to play mother? Don't you agree that you could be confusing *my* son, Miss. Nimms?"

I did not have an answer that would not result in me being thrown out in the cold without a job, or a place to sleep. Suddenly, just like he had before, young Quincy stepped in front of me, his cheeks burning in anger. "Why can't you just leave Miss. Nimms alone? Why do you treat her like she is nothing?" Quincy asked, bawling up his fists, stomping loudly on the floor.

I appreciated it very much when Quincy did such things, but I knew it would only make things worse for the both of us.

Mrs. Shoultz turned to stare at me with those piercing eyes, as she slammed the front door shut, locking Quincy outside, the same way she had done so many times before. I lowered my head, bracing myself for the tongue lashing I would undoubtably receive.

"Do you have children, Miss. Nimms? Do you even know what it takes to raise two young men in a world like this?"

I fought with every fiber of my being to keep myself from crying. I shook my head as I stared down at my shoes. "Your job in this house is to cook and clean, do you understand? It is not your job to mother *my* children! You may *think* that I am some vile, uncaring, cruel mother who cares nothing about her children, but you are wrong, Miss. Nimms. I am trying my darndest to build men, men that will one day follow in the footsteps of their extraordinarily successful father. The problem is, Miss. Nimms, I cannot do that when you are coddling them every single time they start feeling a tad emotional! *They* are children, that is the way *they* are! If you had children of your own, you would know that. Wouldn't you, Miss. Nimms?"

I wanted so badly to walk right out that front door. I had never been disrespected in *this* manner. "I am sorry Mrs. Shoultz. It was not my place to offer *your* son advice in any way. It is just part of being human, I guess."

Mrs. Shoutz had a nose for sarcasm, she smelled it on me like an old hound dog sniffing out a bone. She scoffed at me, turning her head to look up at the large oil painting of the Rocky Mountains on the wall.

"You know, Miss. Nimms, I have always wondered if it was just *your* kind. Maybe, *your* type is just *that* way."

I looked up, unable to stare at my feet any longer. "And what *type* would that be, Mrs. Shoultz?" I had never felt so small, never in all my time working for this horrible woman.

"I am referring to your snarky disposition, Miss. Nimms. Are all your people that way, disobedient and rude to their employers?"

I dropped the tin cleaning bucket to the floor, spilling out my supplies. Mrs. Shoultz turned her head, her brow furrowed, her eyes sharp like circus daggers being thrown at a spinning target.

"I have never." I growled, taking a step forward, despite the venomous glare directed at me. "I have put up with a lot of crap from you over the years, and have let it go, no matter how bad it stung. But one thing I will not tolerate from you, or anyone else in this world, is being treated like less than a human being. I understand your pain, Mrs. Shoultz, I understand more than you will *ever* know. I hear you crying every single night I see the pain you try to hide under all that expensive makeup." She let out a breath, quickly wiping the tear that ran down her pale cheek. She turned away from me, hoping I had not seen.

Mrs. Shoultz sat down on the couch as I poured the both of us a cup of hot tea with a lemon slice on the side. I sat in the armchair across from her, she kept her eyes on the cup in her hands.

"I had two boys of my own once."

She glanced up, locking eyes with me, but only for a moment. I continued as she sipped slowly on her tea. "One of my boys, Jacob, was ten years old when he died."

She stopped drinking her tea, the cup shook in her hand as she placed it on the table in front of her. "I left his older brother Lucious in charge when I went out to find us some food. My husband had gone off and died in the war, left us with nothing but a tiny house in Mississippi, and Baby Jacob in my belly. The first few years were fine, but things progressively grew harder, like they tend to do sometimes. We were short on food and Jacob had gotten real sick. I had to do something, I had to do whatever I could to save my boy. So, I went out, leaving the last bit of the food with the boys before I nailed some boards to the front door of a windowless cabin from the outside. If anyone wanted to get in while I was gone, they would have to fight for it. By the time they *could* get in, Lucious would have a shotgun waiting for them.

"I left, I left my boys there in that cabin, hoping to be back in a few days with enough food to get us through the up coming winter." I wiped my face, feeling a soul crushing pain in my chest and throat.

"Take this." I looked up at Mrs. Shoultz. She held a handkerchief between her fingers.

"Thank you." I nodded, wiping my face. "Well, I guess it's obvious that this story doesn't have the happy ending that I wished it had." I had to use Mrs. Shoultz's handkerchief to wipe my face once more, it was getting harder, considering I had never spoken about my boys to anyone. "I did not make it back in a *few days*, Mrs. Shoultz. I made it back to the cabin three weeks later than I had promised my boys.

"The board, it was still over the door, it did what it was supposed to do, kept unwanted travelers out, but also kept my boys in. I could smell the death in the air from a mile away. I knew what was waiting for me before the cabin was even in my sight."

Mrs. Shoultz stood up, turning away from me, fanning herself with her right hand. "They- they both- both of them?" She asked, her back still facing me as I sat in the huge armchair, forgetting that I had poured myself a cup of tea.

"Yes Madam, both of them. Jacob passed from the sickness. Lucious starved to death. You know what part hurts me the most, Mrs. Shoultz?"

She turned to me, her eyes glassed over, her makeup smeared. "The hardest part was knowing that my oldest boy held out hope, even after his brother died in his bed, even after I had not showed back up. My boy could have used that shotgun, he could have ended his suffering, but he held out hop until his body could not manage it anymore."

To my surprise, Mrs. Shoultz was kneeled beside me, her face resting in my lap. "I am sorry, Miss. Nimms. I am so terribly sorry. My boys so truly fortunate to have someone with your strength in their lives."

Chapter 8

A Light In The Darkness

(Henry Shoultz)

Beethoven's Moonlight Sonata played on the piano downstairs. I knew it was Quincy playing. He was so talented, such an inspiration. "You are smart, Henry, but all this hatred for our family name is holding you back in school. None of those teachers will ever genuinely appreciate your talents. I know it's unfair, but that is just the way things are right now." Quincy put his hand on my shoulder, he tried his best to comfort me with a forced smile, but I knew *that* was all it was.

"Henry Shoultz!" Mrs. Glendale called out to me from the front of the classroom. She had caught me staring out the window that my desk was seated next to.

"Yes, Mrs. Glendale?" I asked, brushing off the euphoria I had felt staring out into the snow-covered small town of Obscurus.

Mrs. Glendale was a stern woman. I had never once seen her smile, not for anything. "Since you're *apparently* too bored to listen to my lecture, maybe you'd like to tell us how the great depression began, and why it was so difficult for anyone to find work."

The only thing *apparent* to me at that moment was that I was not being asked a question, more so being put on the spot because of my family name. Nine of my peers all turned in their chairs to stare at me. Some of them smiling, hoping I would stumble over my words, only to fall flat on my face.

"Well, the great-"

Mrs. Glendale slapped her ruler on the top of her wood desk, scaring the entire class. "Let me correct you before you even begin, Henry. You will start with addressing the educator of this class, which is the one standing up front holding this." She held her ruler up for everyone, but primarily *me*.

"Sorry, Mrs. Glendale. That was quite rude of me. Allow me to start over." My cheeks grew red as everyone once again turned in their chairs to gawk.

"Why don't you stand?" she asked, shooting a devious smile in my direction. I did as I was asked, placing my hands behind my back as well, making sure I stood as straight as my spine would allow.

"Well, Mrs. Glendale, the great depression was the result of the stock market crash of 1929. Even though the economy has slightly improved in some places, we are still facing the effects of the crash. Even now in 1939. The market crashed due to-"

Mrs. Glendale snapped the ruler on her desk once more, scaring the class for a second time. "I'm sure I can take it from there, Mr. Shoultz."

I nodded, then sat back down in my seat. "Due to people like Mr. Alan Shoultz, people who took a gamble without a say from the *regular* folks, folks like my father, my husband, and myself."

I stood up from my chair, this time not placing my hands behind my back. "That is not how, nor why the stock market crashed, Mrs. Glendale. It was to do-"

The ruler snapped on the desk for the third time, but it was expected at this point, not scaring anyone the way it had the first two times. "Sit yourself down, Mr. Shoultz. You were not asked a question, and you most certainly were not asked to stand up! I am the educator, am I not?"

I sat back in my chair; my face looked the way it would after standing out in the freezing cold for an hour straight. "I apologize Mrs. Glendale." I replied, lowering my head in shame. The room was silent for a moment. Only a few whispers amongst my classmates let me know I had not gone def.

"Are you *really* sorry, Mr. Shoultz? Do you know what it means to be sorry? Do you *really* know?" I heard the clacking of Mrs. Glendale's shoes navigating around the others students' desks, her ruler scraping on the tops of them as she walked. The footsteps suddenly stopped. The smell of lady's perfume burned my nostrils. "Place your hands flat on your desk, Mr. Shoultz. I want to show you what it means to be sorry."

I fought back tears, taking a deep breath before looking up at Mrs. Glendale, her hazel eyes piercing me through her reading glasses. "Have you ever felt the consequences of your actions, Mr. Shoultz?"

I wanted to cry but knew I should not. The desk was cold to the touch, I turned my head to look out the window, hoping the beauty that I had become so lost in would save me, even just a little. There was a loud snap, then a sharp pain shot up my fingertips and into my wrists. I focused harder on the inspirational beauty outside the window, the small snowflakes floating peacefully from the heavens, each unique, each helping to build upon one another.

Another loud snap sent another lightning bolt up pain up my hands, this time reaching all the way to my forearms. I squeezed my eyes shut, taking the deepest breath I had ever taken. Another snap, then another, then another. A tear dripped down my cheek, but I would not allow Mrs. Glendale to see it. I would not give her the satisfaction.

"That was for my family." She whispered softly in my right ear.

The moment her footsteps receded, I turned slightly to see if anyone was still staring at me. The only person who still held their sight in my direction was Emily Copper.

"Did it hurt really bad?" Emily asked at recess, approaching me with a sympathetic smile. I looked up at her, still too embarrassed to speak to anyone about what had happened. I glanced down at my fingers, noticing they were now red, with little purple streaks across each of my knuckles.

"Yeah." I muttered, wondering if I should place them deep in the snow at my feet.

"I'm really sorry about that, Henry." Emily added, putting her hand on my shoulder, her smile growing more sympathetic with each awkward passing moment.

"Not as sorry as I am." I responded, trying to make a fist with my left and right hands.

"My big brother has been giving *your* big brother a hard time at school. I'm sorry about that as well."

I stood up from the frozen, snow-covered stump I was sitting on. "What is *that* going to fix, huh, Emily? What are all the sorrys in the world going to fix? I have grown exhausted of everyone telling me how sorry they are. When is it my turn to say sorry? When is my father going to say sorry to people like *your* family? Or people like Mrs. Glendale and her family? I go home every single day to a warm house and lots of food on my plate. What do *you* go home to, Emily?"

Emily bowed her head, twiddling her thumbs together. "*This* is nothing compared to what the people in this town go through every day of their lives!"

Emily looked up as I showed her my swollen fingers.

"Hey Shoultz!" I turned to the sound of a familiar voice behind me. A fist catching me in the face, knocking me down into the snow. "My ma and pa wanted me to let you know how much we appreciate your family!" The voice continued as I stared up at the gray sky, wishing more than anything that I was a bird that could flap its wings and fly away from this place forever. Emily held a handful of snow to my busted lip before we headed back inside to finish school for the day.

I climbed into the backseat of the family car, putting my feet over two larges sacks that were stuffed in the floorboard below. The cigarette smoke was a pleasant reprieve from the stifling air of the cramped schoolhouse.

"What happened?" Quincy asked, motioning to my swollen lip. I shook my head, then turned to watch the school disappear as our car drove over the first hill out of town.

"Mother, what are these bags in the floor?" Quincy asked, poking one of the white sacks with his pointer finger. My mother tossed the rest of her cigarette out through the small crack in the window she had made for the smoke to escape from, before rolling it the rest of the way up. "That is your father's money. Do not mess with it. I had to make a small withdrawal from the bank today, nothing for you boys to worry about."

Quincy and I glanced at each other, then both shrugged our shoulders.

"Mom is so tough, she robbed a bank all by herself, no help from dad." I joked, causing mother to laugh hysterically the rest of the way home.

When we walked through the thick, red oak door, my father stood at the top of the stairs, his arms crossed with a disproving look directed at my mother. "Beatrice, I'd like a word with you in the study after you've directed Miss. Nimms about dinner." My father turned slowly, then walked towards his upstairs study. My mother did not say a word in response. She just stood there, looking up where my father had been standing.

"You go get washed up for dinner, I'll be down in a few moments to speak with Miss. Nimms about what she'll be preparing this evening."

Quincy and I nodded at my mother, before heading to the kitchen to washup. "What do you think father has to speak with mother about, Quincy?" I asked, hiding my swollen fingers from my brother's line of sight as we washed our hands in the kitchen sink.

Quincy and I ate dinner alone that night, sitting across from one another, making faces, laughing at the sound of our echoing voices in the large dining room.

Miss. Nimms poked her head in from the kitchen. "Echo!" she shouted, causing Quincy to laugh so hard that milk came shooting from his nostrils.

I couldn't recall a time that the three of us were so happy, maybe because there was no memory of a time like this happiness before this moment. If there was, I had forgotten entirely.

"What is all this commotion?" My mother stood at the foot of the stairs, just enough to be able to peer into the dining room. "You boys are at the table, not outside on the playground!" Something in my mother's voice sounded different than it had just an hour ago. Mother sounded broken, even a little sad. Luckily Mother couldn't see Miss.

Nimms poking her head out through the kitchen door. I would have hated to hear what she would say about *that*.

I noticed my father walking down the steps past my mother. He didn't bat an eye when she reached out for him. "Alan, please, I could not just-"

My father was out of sight before my mother had chance to finish whatever it was she wanted to say.

"Are you alright, Mother?" Quincy asked concerningly as my mother entered the room, wiping away any signs that she had been crying.

"Mother is fine, Quincy, finish your lamb and spinach. I don't want to hear another word until that plate is spotless. Understood?"

My mother pulled the chair out at the end of the table, the chair my father usually sat in. Mother held out her hand, ringing the little silver bell that she kept on her at all times. "Miss. Nimms!" Mother called out, her little bell ringing obnoxiously.

"Yes, Madam?" Miss. Nimms stuck her head in the room, a back-to-business look on her face as she surveyed the large room.

"I need hot tea, right away." My mother waved her hand dismissively in Miss. Nimms direction.

"Yes, Madam." Miss. Nimms replied, letting the kitchen door swing closed.

"Marry a man with money, my dear mother always said," my mother mumbled to herself as she massaged her temples with her pointer fingers.

Suddenly, there was another bell ringing, but it wasn't the tiny silver one sitting next to my mother.

"Who could that be at this hour?" Mother asked, pushing out her chair, waiting a moment for Miss. Nimms to come scurrying through the kitchen door. "Miss. Nimms, do you plan on answering the door, or must I do it myself?"

There was no response from Miss. Nimms, just the clattering sound of plates and silverware being put away in the kitchen. "I guess I will get it myself!" Mother growled, slamming the little silver bell down on the table, reminding me of Mrs. Glendale and her ruler. A shiver ran down my spine.

"What do you think you will do when you grow-up?" I asked Quincy, who had just taken his final bite of spinach. Quincy looked up, surprised by my inquiry.

"Well, honestly, I'm not sure. If I had to guess, I would say that I would follow in father's footsteps, controlling the mines and whatnot." Quincy scratched the top of his head like a curious ape. "What about you, Henry? What is it that you want to be when you grow-up?"

Unlike Quincy, I was quick to answer. It had a lot to do with the fact that I had stayed up countless nights pondering my future in this world, and where life would take me. "I want to travel the world, helping those in need."

Quincy looked at me puzzled, his left eyebrow slightly arched, the gears in his head turning slowly. "Help people how? Like the peace corps? Why on earth would you want to do something like that? I mean, I get the helping people part, but you have so many advantages, so many resources at your fingertips that not a lot of kids have at your age. Why squander them?"

I *knew* this was the response I would receive from my mother and father, but not from Quincy. Not from the older brother who helped me nurse a baby bird back to health after it fell from its nest, not the brother who was always telling me not to turn out like our mother and father, to be a good person who is willing to do whatever it takes to help those who need helping. What had happened to him? Had Mother and Father dug their claws in so deeply that Quincy felt that following in their footsteps was the only option for him?

"No, not the peace corps. Not that it would matter if that *was* what I meant, right?"

I sat patiently, waiting for Quincy to answer, but he became distracted by mother entering the dining room,

Fathers closest associate in tow. "Boys, Mr. Sinclair will be joining your father for drinks this evening. Go upstairs and get yourselves ready for bed."

Mr. Sinclair stood uncomfortably straight, his face full of wrinkles, his bushy white eyebrows matching the little hair that remained on the top of his head. Quincy and I always made jokes about Mr. Sinclair when no one was around to hear, especially when he would scoff at the two of us for little or no reason whatsoever.

"I'm surprised you allow the children to sit at the table like adults, Beatrice." Mr. Sinclair added, scoffing like an arrogant jackass.

The kitchen door swung open; Miss. Nimms rushed out like the room was on fire. "I'll take those plates, boys. You two head on up. I will get your baths ready once I'm finished down here."

There was another scoff from Mr. Sinclair. "This one is still employed, I see. What a shame. I could have brought a few of mine over to run circles around yours." It was hard not to giggle when my mother turned to us and rolled her eyes, mocking Mr. Sinclair's rude comments.

"Say goodnight to Mr. Sinclair." My mother sighed, pulling my chair back from the table. As rude as Mr. Sinclair was, and as elated as I was to no longer be in the same room with him, I could not shake Quincy's comments from my mind.

"Quincy?" I called out from the tub the moment my older brother walked past the washroom door.

Quincy stopped, leaning back to peak in. "What's up, Henry?" Quincy asked, almost as if I had stopped him in a hurry. I wanted badly to continue our conversation from earlier, to ask if following in Father's footsteps was *really* the outcome that he envisioned for himself.

"Nothing, I'll talk to you about it later."

Quincy smiled, "Are you sure?" he asked, patting the wooden door frame with his hand.

"Yeah, I'm sure. We can talk tomorrow." Quincy smiled, giving me a thumbs-up before disappearing down the hall.

That night I dreamt that I was surrounded by darkness. The only light I could see was a small hole too far away for my hands to reach. Quincy leaned in, calling out my name.

Chapter 9
Necessary Cruelty
(Mr. Sinclair)

I followed Beatrice Shoultz up the stairs after an awkwardly uncomfortable interaction with her filthy little children. The interaction itself made me all the more thankful that my wife and I never had children of our own. Children were vile little creatures that would cry and beg for every ounce of your remaining years, sucking the money from your pocket, all while pretending it's out of necessity.

"Naturally, Alan is in the study." Mrs. Shoultz muttered, a hint of dissatisfaction in her shrill voice.

I never liked Beatrice Shoultz. I told Alan that very thing the first time he introduced me to this *tick* of a woman. "She'll want children, then she will bleed you for all you are worth." I remember warning him on the day of his wedding. I scoffed at the atrocious paintings that Beatrice had hung proudly at the top of the staircase. "Awful, just awful." I shook my head.

Beatrice knocked softly on the door of Alan's study before pushing down on the gold-plated handle. The sweet aroma of cigar smoke brushed against my nose, a feeling of instantaneous comfort settling over my being. "My god, Alan, that cigar smoke is putrid!" Mrs. Shoultz whined, fanning her face with her hand.

"Lucky for your husband and I that this is a man's study, and not the lady's room in your favorite market."

Beatrice turned to me, that same smug look on her bulldog-like face. "I'll leave you to it." She nodded to her husband before exiting the room. The study was lined with several nine-foot-tall bookshelves, each filled with books that I doubt Alan had ever read titles of.

"I hate to pass on the hellos and get straight to business, Alan, but we need to speak on a very pressing matter."

Alan turned away from the large window he stared out of, a half cup of scotch in one hand, a Churchill in the other. "Oh, Charles, I know how much you love the pleasantries of civilized conversation. Why else would I keep you around?" Alan chuckled, always trying to elicit a reaction. "

I am so glad you can find amusement at a time like this, Alan. I personally cannot fathom what is so *laughable*."

Alan took a sip of his scotch, then sat down in the large red-leather chair behind his desk. "A girl died in the Prosper mine yesterday morning. I take matters like *that* very seriously. I was only laughing be-"

"A girl died in the mines yesterday? How is it that I'm only *now* hearing about this? I am your righthand, am I not?" Alan looked surprised, taking another sip of his scotch.

"Oh, my apologies, Charles. I thought the death at the prosper mine was what you came here to talk about."

I began to grow hot under my collar. I yanked at my tie like it was a large snake wrapped tightly around my neck. "Truthfully, Alan. I am here to discuss a more *serious* matter."

Alan folded his hands in front of himself on the desk. "I'm listening, Charles. What pressing matter is more serious than a worker dying in the mine that *we* run?"

I was flabbergasted, truly flabbergasted. Was the missing money from the bank not something to be concerned about? "Alan, I am referring to the very large amount of money that was taken out of the bank vault by your wife."

Alan didn't look all that surprised, which was the truly concerning part. "I am quite aware of what my wife has done, Charles. Quite aware. And *if* you must know, I have already discussed the matter ad nauseum with her. She knows what she did was foolish and unwise. I will have the money placed safely in the new bank in Prosper before the end of the day tomorrow." I had just sat down but was on my feet again so quickly that my knees buckled.

"All of it?!" Alan sensed the surprised tone in my voice. He stood back up to stare out from the window that he had when I entered.

"There is no need to keep my money in the Obscurus. It should not have stayed as long as it has, if I am being frank. No, it is time to move on, no need to sit up here in my ivory tower and watch a dying town squeeze out its final breath."

Alan turned to gauge my reaction; I'm sure he was not disappointed.

"You look surprised, Charles. Did you think I would never leave this place; The place I have built with my own two hands? Did you think I stayed here for sentimental reasons, hoping my daughter would come walking back through the front door?"

An uncomfortable since always fell over the room on the rare occasions that Alan brought up his missing daughter. It never failed.

"I mean, I get why you would want to leave this place from a business perspective, I just never thought it would *actually* happen. Are you going to sell off the house and all the connecting land on which you've been sitting?" I wish

I had not asked such a question. Alan could sense things that most men could not.

"Why? Are you interested in swooping in to buy it all up?" Alan turned once more to gauge my reaction.

"Well, um, yes, I guess I would be interested if you were willing to sell. I would hate to see this beautiful house and all of this land be sold off to some out of towner who wouldn't have a clue what to do with it."

I made sure to keep my emotions in check. Deep down I wanted to jump for joy, the thought of owning this land made my mouth water like a rabid mutt.

"You've always been quite fond of this place, have you not?" Alan asked, pouring himself another glass of scotch. I sat back down in my chair, slouching just a tad.

"It's a nice place, Alan, which is about the extent of it. I have always had a soft spot for owning a big house on a substantial chunk of land. It sure would beat my house at the end of town."

Alan took a sip of his scotch, lighting a match, then holding it to the end of his cigar. "A house like this, it needs to be filled up with a large family, not an old man and his wife who can hardly make it up the front porch without wheezing uncontrollably."

It was not uncommon for Alan to say something insulting to the point of wanting to punch him in the mouth. "I-

I think that is a bit unfair, Alan. I should not be passed by just because I did not want to waste my life with things like children." I turned my head, scoffing loudly. Alan smiled, then stuck his hands in his pockets as he leaned on the corner of his expensive, mahogany desk.

"You have been by my side for a long time, haven't you, Charles? We have been though some pretty nasty fights with some pretty nasty folks with deep pockets and nefarious agendas, haven't we?"

I nodded my head, still trying to nonchalantly show that I was upset.

"You have been vital to my work, especially during all that mess closing down the Obscurus mines. I don't think I would have survived that one without you by my side, keeping me on my toes, making sure that my signature went in all the right places."

I locked eyes with him for a moment, which I knew had been a monumental mistake on my part. Alan was like a shark smelling blood from a mile away, swimming in like a missel with serrated teeth. "I was looking back at a few documents that I had you sign years back; documents that you brought to me the day my daughter disappeared."

It felt as if I had swallowed a strawberry without chewing it first. I remembered bringing Alan those documents, the documents that I had him sign when he was, for a lack of a better term, mentally incapacitated.

"You came here hoping to talk me into signing over my family's old farm. Hoping I would do so with a smile, considering all the help you had been up until that point in my career. But, when you arrived, Beatrice and I were in tears on the front porch, trying desperately to explain our situation to the sheriff and his deputy. You jumped on the opportunity to have me sign a document that *you* claimed pertained to mineral rights for the mines!" He slammed his glass down on his desk, shattering it. My mouth had become dry, my palms became clammy, my heart raced.

"How- How did you-"

"How did I find out?" Alan interrupted, grabbing a sheet of paper from his desk drawer. "You kept the documents in my safe at the bank, you moronic dunce!" Alan slammed the paper down on his desk, soaking it in spilt scotch. "You have had control over that parcel of land for all these years, and for what? *What* have you used it for?" Alan asked, his curiosity always getting the better of him.

I stood on my feet, Alan's eyes widening with surprise. "What do you care? Neither you, nor anyone else in your family has visited that old farm, not even once, since the day your parents died and left it to you. I watched it go to waste, the same way you have watched that town!" I pointed out the window towards Obscurus. "If someone came along and asked to buy that town, would you let them? Or would you shrug them off just so you could continue watching it rot away?"

For the first time since I have known Alan Shoultz, he was speechless.

"My Daughter. Did you take my daughter, Charles?"

I turned to see Beatrice standing in the now opened doorway, tears streaming down her cheeks.

"No! I would never do something like that! Never!" I protested, not believing that I was being asked such outlandish questions by my boss's wife.

I turned to Alan, putting my hands up defensively. "You *know me*, Alan. You know I would never to do anything like that to your family, especially over some silly old, run-down farm!" The room was silent for a few moments. So silent you could almost hear that heartbeat of the little boy listening in from the upstairs hallway. "You have to believe me, Alan. Please say that you do!"

He didn't respond, he just turned to stare out the window once more. I walked out the front door of the Shoultz mansion after signing the farm back over to Alan and his family. A hard slap in my face from Mrs. Shoultz was enough validate that after tonight, I was no longer employed by Shoultz Industries.

Two days following my termination there was a loud knock on my door. Two police officers with billy-clubs stood on my front porch, one of them holding a pair of shackles. After a few hours in a small room and some hard right hooks to my face and stomach, I told them where Susanna Shoultz was.

"The silo, she is buried in the silo."

Chapter 10
The Silo
(Alan Shoultz)

"What is it, Alan? The kids are just now home from school and the drive has worn me down," my wife asked, following me into my upstairs study at my request.

"Close the door behind you. We need to talk."

Beatrice did as I asked, closing the door softly. "I must say, Alan, you of all people wanting to talk in private is a tad concerning."

I knew I had been a shoddy husband over the course of our marriage, and I knew I was not the easiest person to speak to, especially about a home or family matter. My wife could be an overbearing woman at times, being the wife of one of the richest men in the country could put some extra weight on one's mental health, even more so when the man you are married to had to make very tough, life altering decisions. I was never the type of man to make excuses for the way that I was, or for the type of man I had grown to become. But Beatrice knew, she knew what this lifestyle was capable of turning you into, the many masks you had to wear in order to appear sane in a world that would rip you to shreds without a moment's notice.

Through all this, my wife remained strong. She kept our children strong; she kept our house from crumbling under the weight of my worst decisions in life. And for that, I owed her the truth, the whole truth.

"Tell me, Alan. What is this about? Tell me before I drop dead from the paranoia you are unjustly causing in this moment."

I poured a glass of scotch from my private collection, the collection I never shared with guests, or even close business associates. "Beatrice, I know that you pulled the money from the bank. I had a very lengthy conversation with Mr. Garet from the bank about it. Before you place your hands on your hips and roll your eyes, just know I am not upset, nor am I the least bit angry with you."

Beatrice acted as if she was about to place her hands on her hips anyway but seemed to decide against doing so. "Alright, if *that* isn't what this is about, *what* is it?"

I took a sip from my glass. The warm liquor ran down my throat, the sweet taste of aged wood and subtle fruit calmed me, which I needed *now* more than ever. "In the vault, mixed in with the money, there were some documents that I had signed years back. Documents that I never meant to sign."

Beatrice looked confused, stepping further into the room.

"There was one document that was dated the day that Susana disappeared."

Beatrice no longer appeared confused as she inched closer, placing her hands on the back of a chair in front of my desk. Looking at my wife, I couldn't believe how neglectful I had been over the years, hiding out in this room as if it was a bomb shelter and I was just waiting for the world outside to end under a cloud of black smoke.

"I know it is tough to recall anything other than the pain and confusion we were both feeling that day, but do you remember Charles stopping by with some paperwork shortly after Susana's disappearance?"

Beatrice shook her head. I knew all she could see was our daughter's face and nothing more.

"I don't understand, Alan." My wife sighed, shaking her head, trying to block out the painful memories that she had suppressed over these years.

"Charles had me sign a few documents that I needed to sign, having to do with mineral rights in the mine. But there was one document I signed that allowed Charles to take my mother and father's farm. I must have singed it in a hurry, not bothering to read over it like I would any other day."

Beatrice turned quickly away from me, fighting back the tears, fighting back the rage that she had *every* right to feel. "That bastard. He is your closest associate. You've trusted him for years!"

I nodded in agreement, stepping forward to take my wife's hands in mine. "He called earlier to say that he has to stop by tonight to discuss an important matter. I am almost certain that it has to do with the money being taken from the bank. When Charles arrives here tonight I-" I felt my wife's grip tighten, fire burning behind her eyes. "When Charles arrives, we will play it off like any other night. I promise on every ounce of love I have for you, and our children, I will find the underlying cause of this."

Beatice nodded reluctantly but agreed to do as I asked.

My closest associate. My dearest, longest lasting friend, walked out the front door for the final time that night.

"You bastard! Where is Susana!? Where is my daughter!?" Beatrice dropped to her knees in the foyer, screaming at the top of her lungs. I tried my hardest to console her as she cried in my arms. I looked to the top of the steps where my two sons stood, their little faces hidden behind the banister. Miss. Nimms quickly ran up to them, leading them carefully back to their rooms. We would tell them after the chaos had settled, explaining that they once had a sister who was no longer with us. Being the bright boys that they were, they would come to understand in time.

Weeks had passed since we buried Susana, our daughter, who had been taken before she had a chance to experience the good life had to offer. Beatrice seemed almost at peace now that the weight of not knowing had been removed from our shoulders. It was bittersweet, I guess, knowing she wasn't suffering, locked away somewhere, crying out for us.

Miss. Nimms and my wife seemed to form some sort of bond over the past few days. From what I've been told, they sat down together one afternoon and decided to chat. I'm not sure about what exactly, but whatever it was seemed to form a relationship between the two of them.

"Father?" I was shaken from a daze by my oldest son, Quincy, curiosity in his voice as he pointed out the large window in the living room towards my parents' old farm. "Mother said that you lived there once. Is that true? Is that where you grew up?"

I looked out over the hills, the old silo sticking up over them, a grim reminder of recent tragedy. "Sure is. I lived there with my mother and father when I was a boy, moved out when I was just a few years older than you are now."

Quincy turned, putting his hands to the cold glass, his breath fogging up a little spot at the very bottom. "Can we go there? I would really like to see it up close after all these years of staring at it from our family room window."

A feeling of anxiousness fell over me like a spirit's cold embrace. "Actually, I had recently decided to have it torn down, considering it isn't used anymore. Maybe we can put in some horse stables in the spring. You and I could learn to ride."

Quincy's head dropped against the glass in disappointment. "To be honest, Son. Your father does not have many fond memories of that place. When you look out that window and see the farm, you see the unknown, something new for you to explore. For me, it's a grim reminder of a time I would much rather forget." I placed my hand on Quincy's shoulder, hoping he would understand.

That night I found myself unable to sleep, tossing and turning, thinking about that dreadful place I once called home.

"Get in there! I don't want to see your face until the entire thing is empty, you hear?" My father spat a long, sticky sting of tobacco spit. "If you are going to be the one running this place one day, you best know how to take care of it."

My father pushed me from behind. I fell onto the silo floor, rotten grain like quicksand under my hands and knees. "But, Pa, there are rats living in here!" I called out before he limped away, mumbling something unintelligible under his breath. It took hours for me to shovel out the old animal feed, filling wheelbarrow after wheelbarrow of rotted, grain and discolored corn. My back ached, my hands covered in blisters, my chest aching from trying to catch my breath.

"Pa, I've finished cleaning out the silo!" I called out, limping into the house, pulling off my worn-out boots.

"That no good son of a-" my father turned to see me standing in the hallway outside the kitchen, my mother's eye swollen from being punched during one of Pa's night terrors. "Who's he going to leave it to? Him?" Pa asked, turning, and pointing in my direction with a crumbled-up letter in his hand.

"It's Theodore's choice. There's nothing we can do about it."

Theodore was my uncle on my mother's side, a rich and powerful man who owned and operated the local mine; the mine that my father once owned. "He rips me off, taking the mine from me for peanuts after all the years I spent running the place. I was the type of owner to get down there and work with my men, not some pencil pushing jackass like your worthless excuse of a brother!" He slammed his hand down on the table before getting up and limping out through the back door.

My Uncle Theodore had offered my father a very handsome amount of money for the Obscurus mine, even drawing up a contract to make it official. Little did my father know, he agreed to small monthly payments from Uncle Theodore over the course of thirty years.

"What was all that about?" I asked my mother, sitting down in the chair across the table from her.

She glanced up for a moment before burying her face in her hands like she had been doing for the past five minutes. "Your Uncle Theo is sick He's leaving you the mine when he passes. I reckon your Pa thought he would return it to *him* instead."

My heart raced, the excitement I felt was impossible to put into words. The thought of running the mine and never having to deal with the pain of running this *useless* farm was enough to make me jump up and down for joy, though I remained seated for obvious reasons.

"It looks like you'll be joining your uncle in the next few days at his home on the outskirts of town. He'll be teaching you all you'll ever need to know. And if I can offer a small piece of advice, Son, you learn all you can and then some." My mother reached across the table, placing her hand on top of mine. "You deserve more than this life, and you are a whole lot smarter than that old fool outside." She nodded towards the door my father had barged out of. "You Grandfather would be turning in his grave if he knew what you Pa had done selling the mine like that." She rolled her eyes, patting my hands before getting up to throw some more wood in the stove.

A day or so after, I found myself shoveling manure from the bull pen, the blisters on my hands popping one at a time. It was silly to own a single bull and a bunch of useless goats. No wonder my father was incapable of running a business.

"Boy!"

I turned to see Pa limping over towards the pen. He was using an old stick as a cane, leaning heavily on his right side. "Did your ma tell you all about the letter from your no-good thieving uncle?" He against the fence; brown tobacco spit stained his chin.

"Yes Sir." I answered, nodding my head.

Pa nodded as well, looking over his shoulder before staring back at me. "You aren't doing diddly squat with that mine. The second that thief dies, you are going to sign that property over to me, understand? You are going to have your hands full running this farm when you're old enough. You will not have the time to be running some silly old mine."

I leaned my pitchfork against the stall that held Samson, a big mean bull that my father kept around, even after smashing Pa's leg in between his massive head and a fence post. "We'll have some cows soon, that bull will come in handy." Pa always claimed, knowing damn well he would never spend the money.

"What is there to *run* in this place? This isn't even a farm. It's a chunk of useless land with useless livestock. Heck, even some hens would make this place a little money. Why not get some of those? And as for the coal mine, I want to try my hand at it. I bet I could learn a lot from a smart businessman like Uncle Theodore."

I had never seen the expression on my father's face that I was seeing at that moment. It was a look someone would make when they felt stabbed in the back. Little did I know, I would see that look many times, from many different people in the years to follow. Uncle Theodore was a tough, hardnosed businessman, who crushed anyone who dared get in his way.

"You ungrateful little cretin!" My father growled, throwing his leg over the wooden fence that separated the two of us. I knew if Pa was to get ahold of me, I would surely be beaten senseless, or worse. "Come here and tell me how *useless* this farm is, boy!" Pa grabbed the bullwhip that hung near the water trough. "Get over here, boy! It is about time you learned about respect, something you are never going to learn working with that lousy, thief uncle of yours!"

Without a second thought, I kicked the latch on Samson's pen, causing it to swing open wide enough for the two-thousand-pound bull to charge out, right towards my father.

"It's a tragedy, a real tragedy. The man died bitter, and angry." I looked over at Uncle Theo as we stood in front of my father's casket. "Your grandfather on your daddy's side, he knew how to run a coal mine. Your daddy on the other hand, not so great." Uncle Theo chuckled, before coughing loudly into his handkerchief.

"The damn coughing never stops, no matter what they give me. I tell you, there is a curse on the coal mines in this area. That's the only way I can explain all the crap that goes on." He showed me the specks of blood on his white handkerchief before stuffing it back down into his pocket.

"I wonder is Ma is going to be okay by herself. I hate the thought of leaving her there all alone." Theo and I turned to my mother, she sat in the front row, chatting with Dolores White, a neighbor who lived a few miles down the road.

"She'll be fine, I will make sure she is taken care of, I promise." Uncle Theo patted me on the back.

Over the years I learned everything Theo knew about business, state laws, getting in with the right folks. I continued learning, continued growing, even after Uncle Theo passed away. By the time I was twenty-one, I was one of the richest, most powerful men in the country, running the coal mines in Obscurus, Kingstown, and New Hawk. My fortune grew much like my reputation, even more so than Uncle Theo's ever had.

"You want to see a movie?" I asked my lady friend as she held on tightly to my arm, the two of us walking down the busy streets of Obscurus on a Friday night. "Hi there, Mr. Shoultz!" People would tip their hats and smile as they passed.

"I'd love to see a movie!" Beatrice Falcone replied, smiling up at me, the world in the palm of her hand.

"If that's what my girl wants, that's what she will get!" I smiled back, kissing her softly on the cheek.

"Alan! Alan, wake up!" I felt myself being shaken by the shoulders. "What? What is it?" I woke up in bed, rubbing my eyes so that the room would come into focus, Beatrice still holding tightly to my shoulders. "There are people outside of our house. I think it's the town!" It took me a few moments to register what Beatrice was screaming about, then I heard the angry mob just below my bedroom window.

"Alan Shoultz! Get out here and face us like a man, you damn coward!" An angry man's voice called up so loudly that it was almost as if he were standing in the room next to us.

"Phone the sheriff, tell him to get up here as quickly as possible!" I ordered my wife, pulling myself quickly out of bed and pulling on my silk robe.

I went to the window and pulled back the curtains, torches held by an angry mob lit up the darkness. I unlatched the window, pushing it open with my knuckles. "What is the meaning of this!" I called down on the mob, only recognizing a few faces under the flickering torches.

"You, and people like you, have sucked the life from this town, leaving us to go without food, without heat, without our livelihoods!" a man I recognized as Lucas Simmions, shouted up at me, waving his torch in the air above his head.

"I did not take a thing from Obscurus, or the folks that live there! I closed the mine, which is it. I told every single man and woman who was laid off that you would have a job waiting for you in Prosper, you would just have to wait until we built enough homes to accommodate all of you! You make me out to be a monster, when that is the furthest thing from reality!"

My throat grew raw in the cold winter air as I shouted at the top of my lungs. The large crowd muttered to one another, too low for me to make out what they were saying. "So, we are all supposed to uproot our lives and move to another town, all because you sucked all the resources from this one? Most of us were born here. There is a cemetery full of our loved ones. Do you suppose we just dig them up and take them with us before you bulldoze the place?"

I wanted to pull my window shut and climb back into my warm bed, pretending this was all just a bad dream. "All of that will be taken care of with the upmost respect. You have my word. I will not bulldoze over your dead loved ones."

I thought about the little spot in Prosper where we buried Susana, then about my mother, my father, and Uncle Theo buried here in Obscurus. Did I plan to bulldoze over them?

"Your *word*, it doesn't mean a thing to us!" A woman called out from the angry crowd.

"Look, we can have a town meeting at the old courthouse where we can discuss all of this, but please, go home. Go home to your children and let me do the same." The crowd grew angrier, throwing rocks at the front door.

"Father? What is happening? What is that noise?" I turned to see my sons standing in the doorway, rubbing their eyes, scared, and confused.

"It's okay, boys. Go on back to bed. Your mother and I have grownup stuff to deal with right now, okay?" I considered holding Henry up to the window in hopes the crowd would feel sympathetic, but I didn't want to frighten my son further.

Miss. Nimms came running down the hall in her sleeping gown, grabbing both boys, leading them back to their rooms. I turned back to look at the angry mob just as Beatrice re-entered the bedroom. "They are throwing things at the house. What is wrong with these savages?" My wife asked, joining me at the window.

"Burn it down!" A man shouted, throwing his fiery torch at the downstairs window.

The sound of glass shattering made my wife and I run for our children's rooms, screaming for them to follow us downstairs and out the backdoor. We watched from the freezing snow as the house I had built, our belongings, all of it turned to ash in the towering inferno that lit up the endless holler for two full nights. I looked over at Miss. Nimms as she wrapped the boys in a fur blanket, then at my wife as she cried on my shoulder.

"The money. It was all in my study." Beatrice went quiet, just like we *all* had.

Chapter 11
I'll Never Forget The Winter Of 1939
(Quincy Shoultz)

All these years later, and the only thing I could think about was my little brother, Henry. It's been eleven years since the accident, eleven years since the fire that burned away everything my parents had built.

My parents were never the same after Henry's passing. Something in them changed, making them cold and bitter, even towards me. After the fire, my father sold off the coal mines and the rest of the property my family owned, giving my parents enough extra income to buy them a lovely place to retire in New York City.

I lived with them up until I was old enough to move out, which didn't seem to bother them the way it did *most* parents. We don't speak much except for holidays and the occasional birthday. From what I've heard, my mother filed for divorce a few months back.

I took some time off work last year to go and pay a visit to the town of Obscurus. It was amazing seeing a town that spent years on the brink of death thriving like nothing had ever happened. The streets were packed with families on their way to visit the city park, restaurants full of delighted customers, the sky blue without a cloud in sight. It was like stepping into another world.

"Howdy stranger!" I was greeted warmly as I walked past the local hardware store by an old man being led inside by the prettiest girl I had ever seen.

"Are you stopping by my father's shop?" the young woman asked, holding the door open.

"Oh, um, no, actually. I was just heading over to diner to get myself something to eat. Do you recommend anything on the menu?" I asked, feeling my cheeks turn a shade of red.

"Well, they serve a pretty good cheesesteak." She suggested, shrugging her shoulders.

"I'll definitely have to try that out. This may seem forward, but would you care to join me?" I screamed at myself on the inside, never being particularly good at this sort of thing. The young woman looked over her shoulder and into her father's shop.

"You go on, Sweetie, you deserve a break after walking your old dad around all day." The old man behind the counter joked, waving his daughter away with a smile.

"My name is Quincy, Quincy Shoultz." I had almost forgotten my name, something that was hard to do in the town of Obscurus, especially for the son of the man who nearly killed it.

"Quincy Shoultz?" the beautiful woman stopped in her tracks right before we entered the front door of the diner. "You don't remember me, do you?"

I felt like a total dunce. How could anyone forget a face like *that*? "I'm terribly sorry, I don't recognize you. Did we know each other once?"

She stared at me for another moment, I guess hoping that it would somehow click. "Lana, Lana Kingsly. We went to school together."

Just like that, it hit me. "Lana! You were the one who saved me from getting my face pounded in by Edward Copper that day back in thirty-nine." I pictured Lana standing with her hands on her hips, a disapproving look on her face.

"That's me." She smiled as I opened the door for her.

Sitting in that diner, Lana and I talked and talked, the hours flying by like minutes. "I am so glad that that I ran into you." I admitted, walking with Lana back to the hardware store.

"It was really nice seeing you." Lana responded, wrapping her arms around me, then kissing my cheek before rejoining her father in his store.

Lana and I would get married a year later, buying our own place in the heart of Obscurus. Later down the road we had our first son in April of 1952. We named him Henry.

I never re-visited the old mine, nor the place where the Shoultz mansion once sat. I decided to leave the past in the past and focus on the bright future that lay ahead of me.

Lana's father later passed, leaving the hardware store to us. One winter day I was working the store by myself, thinking about closing up early and heading home before the snow trapped me inside. The bell rang on the front door as I was finishing sweeping up a pile of sawdust. I looked up to see Miss. Nimms standing in the doorway, a big smile on her wrinkled face. "Hey there, Quincy." She whispered, reaching out as I rushed over to hug her. "I see you are doing pretty well for yourself, Sweetie. You have no idea how happy that makes me."

Miss. Nimms and I sat down on a couple of stacks of horse feed, reminiscing about how great of a kid Henry was, and what he would be doing now if he were still around.

"I went and got myself married to some old fool out in Kentucky, but it didn't last too long. Decided to move back up here to spend my final days. As much crap as your momma gave me, and all I put up with living in that house, those were still the best days of an extraordinarily long life."

I smiled and said my goodbyes to Miss. Nimms as I walked her to the door, not knowing it would be the last time we would ever speak. Lana and I had Her buried in Mississippi next to her two sons.

My mother and father eventually passed as well. Oddly enough, only three days apart. I was unable to make it to either of their services due to the birth of my beautiful daughter, Danielle Shoultz.

My life felt like a dream, sometimes scary, sometimes beautiful. One thing that I'll never forget, even sitting here as an old man on my front porch, watching my grandkids pile out of the car when they visited for the holidays. I would never forget the winter of 1939.

About the Author

Stuart Drake was born on the Kodiak Islands of Alaska on September 11th, 1991. Obscurus, 1939 is his debut novel outside of the horror genre. Stuart lives with his wife and two sons in Salem, Kentucky, writing every chance he gets.

Made in the USA
Middletown, DE
03 September 2024